Do Lord Remember Me

Praise for Julius Lester and *Do Lord Remember Me*

"As *Roots* did for us all a decade ago in its melodramatic yet undeniably epic fashion, *Do Lord Remember Me* does in its smaller way for a generation of American blacks: it returns dignity to a history that had been forgotten in an angrier, more activist time."
—*Chicago Sun-Times*

"Julius Lester . . . is foremost among . . . black writers who produce their works from a position of historical strength."
—*The New York Times Book Review*

"Lester writes with . . . poetic ease, evoking a strong emotional response in the reader. . . . *Do Lord Remember Me* celebrates memory's validation of a life fully lived."
—*The Washington Post*

"*Do Lord Remember Me* is . . . packed with stories of power and substance, beautifully told."
—*Boston Herald*

"*Do Lord Remember Me* [is] distinguished by a simplicity and clarity that seem exactly right."
—*People*

"BITTERSWEET, GENEROUS, EXQUISITELY CRAFTED. . . . A FINE, BEAUTIFUL NOVEL, simple in its language and design, but deep and complex in the way it shows good people paying a price trying to stay good—and alive in a time of great evil."
—*Newsday*

A Novel by

Julius Lester

Do Lord Remember Me

WASHINGTON SQUARE PRESS
PUBLISHED BY POCKET BOOKS NEW YORK

This novel is a work of fiction. Names, characters, places and incidents are either the product of the author's imagination or are used fictitiously. Any resemblance to actual events or locales or persons, living or dead, is entirely coincidental.

A Washington Square Press Publication of
POCKET BOOKS, a division of Simon & Schuster, Inc.
1230 Avenue of the Americas, New York, N.Y. 10020

Published by arrangement with Holt, Rinehart and Winston
Library of Congress Catalog Card Number: 84-3845

ISBN: 0-671-60707-3

First Washington Square Press trade paperback printing May, 1986

10 9 8 7 6 5 4 3 2 1

WASHINGTON SQUARE PRESS, WSP and colophon are
registered trademarks of Simon & Schuster, Inc.

Printed in the U.S.A.

For
MY MOTHER

Contents

Afternoon

The Reverend Joshua Smith, Sr. was born November 5, 1900 in Ouichitta, Mississippi.

He stared at what he'd written. It was a simple statement of fact. Or it was supposed to be. But it wasn't. Reverend Smith's eyes narrowed. Couldn't he remember even when he was born?

He rubbed his cheek as if it were a talisman that would yield the memory as elusive now as life itself was becoming, but his fingers found only the stubble of gray hair. His hands had trembled so that morning, he hadn't been able to hold the electric razor steady. Some mornings he steadied his wrist with his left hand, but not that morning. He preferred the clean stroke of a blade, but his hands shook so now that he couldn't put on shaving cream. The last time he had tried, more had gone on his lips than around them.

"What'd you do that for, Reverend Smith?" she'd asked from the doorway of the bathroom.

"I didn't do it on purpose," he snapped, not knowing she'd been there leaning on her cane.

"I wish you'd let me call the visiting nurse service and have them send somebody around every day to help you with things like that," she continued, concern in her voice.

"If you'd just let me alone, I'd be all right." He glared, a glob of shaving cream dropping from his upper lip onto the lapel of his bathrobe. He looked down at it and then at her. "I'm sorry," he mumbled.

She nodded, as if it were foolish to be sorry for what couldn't be helped. "Your breakfast is almost ready," she said, before turning and walking away.

It didn't matter now. Death had shown him its face twice and the last time it hadn't been so frightening or ugly. It was only his fear that had made Death ugly.

As if waking from a heavy sleep, he saw the sheet of paper at which his eyes were staring, and, for an instant, didn't recognize the handwriting, the words trembling on the page as if shaking in a cold wind.

He read the sentence again. It was wrong, but what was right? It was like that more and more, the seeing but not recognizing, the recognition without knowledge. There were old people, like her brother, Earl, who didn't know what year they were living in, didn't know that they were no longer who they had been.

With some effort he pushed the chair back from the desk and opened the center drawer. A manila folder lay atop a clutter of pads, pens, paper clips, and pencils and he placed it on the desk. Laboriously moving the chair forward, he opened the folder and looked at the first sentence of the obituary he'd written last week.

Reverend Joshua Smith was born November 5, 1900 in Ouichitta, Mississippi.

That was wrong, too. He read all three pages of the obituary and was pleased that everything else seemed correct. He turned the three stapled pages facedown on the empty side of the folder and looked at the next obituary, one he'd written last month.

The Reverend Joshua Smith, Sr. was born November 5, 1897 in Ouichitta, Mississippi.

He read the sentence again and nodded. That was right. He closed the folder of previously written obituaries and pushed it to the side. He drew a wavering line through "1900" and with an almost childlike intensity and concentration, wrote "1897" above, trying to make the lines and curves of the numbers as sturdy as youth. Shaking his head, he dropped the sheet of paper into the wastebasket beside his chair.

Opening the drawer to his right, he took another sheet of paper and wrote again:

The Reverend Joshua Smith, Sr. was born November 5, 1897 in Ouichitta, Mississippi.

That was wrong! He was born in 1900. He started to drop the sheet of paper in the wastebasket and then stopped. Carlotta was born in 1897! Twenty-seven years old when they married, but she'd put twenty-one on the marriage license. Then she waited fifty years to tell him, waited until he had a stroke and didn't know if he'd ever walk again, if he lived.

The doctor said he was making good progress, considering that the week before he couldn't even wiggle his toes. Who wanted to live when toes that wiggled like crippled fish were a sign of life?

The first night after he was brought home from the hospital, he lay in bed, glad that if he was going to die, it would be at home. Dying was less alien if he slipped into it from familiar odors.

She was sitting on the edge of her bed, reading a magazine on her lap. He turned his head and stared at her and it was as if all their fifty-six years were molded into a tiny heart which pulsated weakly and irregularly now and he had to talk about that shrinking and wrinkled heart before it was dust and imperfect memory. He started telling her how young and pretty she looked from the pulpit that Sunday morning. It was his first church, a little whitewashed frame building in the middle of a field and he was nervous, knowing that everybody was waiting to see if this man as black as a thousand midnights in a cypress swamp could preach. He was even more nervous when she walked in. What was a white girl doing in a colored church, black hair

5

spilling over her shoulders and down her back like a silken waterfall? Beside her walked a white woman with dark brown hair wrapped in a ball at the back of her head. He knew they couldn't be white, not in Pine Grove, Arkansas, in 1923, but he was still afraid to look at her.

"I wasn't as young as you thought," she interrupted.

"What're you talking about?"

"I'm three years older than you." She didn't look up from the magazine and said it in that dry way of hers, as if he didn't have feelings she was supposed to care about. "You know how it was back then," she continued, still not caring to touch him with her eyes. "If a woman got to be twenty-seven and wasn't married, everybody called her an old maid. And I figured you wouldn't be any different. If I was twenty-seven and still single, you would've thought there was something wrong with me."

Maybe it wouldn't have hurt as much if she hadn't laughed.

"What's so funny?" he demanded, wishing he could rise up from the bed and slap her.

"Oh, nothing," she said, still cackling. "But it is kind of funny, you thinking you were the oldest all these years."

"I don't see anything funny about it."

"Wouldn't expect you to."

He wiped at his eyes.

"Would you have married me if I'd told you the truth?" she asked, looking at him for the first time.

"Of course I would have," he said, his voice weak and unconvincing to himself even.

"I'm glad I didn't put you to the test back then," she concluded, closing the magazine and dropping it to the floor.

He sniffed and his attention returned to the sentence he'd written. He changed the period to a comma and resumed writing.

the seventh child of Charles and Mary (Collins) Smith.

He put down the pen, closed his eyes, and tried to remember them. Dallas was the oldest. Then came Pecola, who died of diphtheria before he was born. Alice died the year he was born. She'd been five. Pauline was little when she died. Myra died when he was seven and Sue Ann when he was eight. Samuel and Louis were born after him, six and ten years later. Nine children and only the four boys lived to be grown. Two were left now. Soon there'd be just one.

He smiled, pleased that he remembered all of them without having to pause and think. He might forget where he put his house key, but he could probably remember on which side of the bureau he'd laid it fifty years ago. Dying wasn't nothing but going back to the beginning.

The first box he'd ever made was the one he helped Poppa with for Myra. It was only four foot long, because she had always been tiny. She died in the night. He was awake in the dark listening to Poppa praying and crying and then, way up in the night, Momma shrieked and he knew Myra had died.

He got out of bed and Sue Ann whispered, "Where you going, Joshua?"

He didn't answer but climbed over her, took off his nightshirt, slipped on his pants and a shirt, and walked across the porch to the other side of the house where Myra had been sleeping in his parents' room since she'd taken sick.

Poppa was sitting in the rocking chair staring out the front window into the night. Momma lay across the bed atop Myra whose eyes were open and looking through the ceiling at the stars. He pulled his mother away gently. "She's with God now, Momma. It's all right. She's laying in Jesus' arms."

He led his mother to the front porch and sat her in the

swing, stroking her arms. As first light eased up from the horizon soft as a cloud, he heard noises from the barn and in a moment, Poppa came riding past on the wagon, hitting at the mule with the whip.

Joshua left his mother and returned to the bedroom. Poppa had closed Myra's eyes, laid her straight on the bed, and folded her hands at her waist. Joshua sat down on the edge of the bed and stroked the face of his favorite sister. He didn't let himself ask God why she had died. He didn't let himself be angry with God for taking her away from him. She was with Jesus and didn't have to worry about sin now. He stroked her face, biting his lower lip, and then went to the other side of the house and woke Sue Ann.

"You got to get up and get breakfast started."

"Leave me alone," she muttered, turning her back to him.

"You get up and do it right now!"

"Don't you be telling me what to do!" she yelled, sitting up. "I'm older than you. You can't be bossing me around."

He was only seven years old, but Poppa said there was something about him that was different and he felt it at that moment as rage hardened his body and mind as he looked at his older and only sister now acting childish while Momma was sitting on the porch like she wouldn't ever move again and Poppa was on his way to the lumberyard to get wood for the box and Myra wasn't going to laugh anymore and make them happy and how Momma was going to have another baby soon and how he was going to have to get the eggs from the hen house and feed the chickens and then go to the field and start picking the pole beans because they were ready and pole beans didn't know nothing about sisters dying and he slapped Sue Ann and it wasn't a little boy's hand against the side of her face but something as rigid as a board and hard as stone. "You get up and get up right now!"

A year later she was dead. It was almost the same time of year. She came in from the field complaining of being hot and no one paid her any mind. Poppa didn't go to town for the white doctor because he was hot and tired, too. The next morning when Momma said that Sue Ann might have the galloping fever, Poppa went but it was the day after that before the white doctor came. It was too late then and the doctor said that niggers were too triflin' to even send for the doctor like they oughta and a week later she was dead. Poppa didn't sit in the rocker staring at the night this time. He left the house and Joshua thought he was going to get the pine boards from the lumberyard but he wasn't back by sundown and when he hadn't come by sunup the next morning, Joshua took the other mule from the barn and rode to Brother Emory's to borrow his wagon and went to the lumberyard.

He made Sue Ann's box himself. The hardest part was carrying her and putting her in it, because it was just him and Momma and Momma couldn't carry for crying. "I ain't got no more girl chillen," she said over and over. "All my girl chillen is dead. God took'em all from me."

Finally they got Sue Ann in the box and Joshua nailed on the top. By then Brother Emory had come with some of the neighbors and they put the box in the wagon and Joshua helped his mother onto the seat and they drove to the colored cemetery in town.

Joshua didn't feel right about no words being said over his sister, but Poppa was the preacher and hadn't nobody been able to find him. Brother Simpson, who said he'd dug every grave for colored in Ouichitta since back in slavery, was finishing with Sue Ann's when Joshua hollered "Whoa!" to the mule. Some of the men got ropes and slung them around the box and as they lowered it into the ground, Joshua stepped to the edge of the grave, lowered his head, and said, "Our Father, You gave her life and we give her back to Thee. We don't understand why, but You do. Dry the tears of them that weep. Hold them in the palm of Your hand, Father, until that glorious day when we all meet again in Heaven. Amen."

He took a handful of dirt and threw it on top of the box and Brother Simpson began shoveling on the rest of the dirt as the people started singing, "Soon I will be done with the troubles of this world. . . ."

Late that night Poppa came home. He was a tall, lean man, skin as black and sleek as crow feathers. Joshua knew from the redness in his eyes that he'd been drinking. Josh wasn't black like his granddaddy, but was as tall and drank about as much, probably.

That was how sin worked. It skipped a generation and Reverend Smith had seen the sign watching his firstborn, Josh, shoot up like a clump of ragweed. His lips might've been thin like his mother's, but he walked in that loose-jointed way like Poppa had, as if he'd rather dance to where he was going.

But Poppa had stopped walking like he was surrounded by dance music after Sue Ann died. His legs didn't seem to have no more strength than the tops of green onions as he stumbled up the steps and across the porch night after night. Joshua would awaken in the bed where he'd slept with Sue Ann and listen to Poppa struggle to his feet, muttering curses, sometimes under his breath, sometimes shouting, listen to him fall against the house, a sudden silly chuckle disturbing the night stillness, until finally, he found the doorknob and lurched into the dog run that separated the two parts of the house. Some nights he fell onto the porch and Joshua waited for the chuckle or the curse, and when neither came, he would get out of bed and go outside, and kneel beside the prone, foul body.

"Get up, Poppa," he'd whisper. "Come on. Get up."

Sometimes he would and other times he couldn't and Joshua would have to leave him for the morning sun.

But no matter how many nights he came home drunk during the week, Poppa was always up with the sun on Sunday mornings. Momma stopped going to church after Sue Ann died, but Poppa would be the first one there, and every Sunday morning as Joshua stood beside his father at the front door to the church, watching him say "Blessings on you" to each person as he or she came in, Joshua thought that maybe this week Poppa would be Poppa all through the week.

He sat on the first bench, looking up at Poppa as he danced back and forth across the pulpit, his arm thrust high into the air like the steeple on the white folks' church, shouting, "God don't like ugly! God don't like sin and if you think He do, you and hellfire gon' be good friends all through eternity!" And he'd laugh and Joshua would smile and know that this week he wouldn't have to lie in the darkness and hear Poppa screaming and slapping Momma, because once he'd asked Poppa how come he laughed when he was preaching and Poppa had said, "Son, it seems like sometimes I get so filled with loving God, I just got to laugh," and Poppa was laughing and dancing and Brother Emory shouted, "Preach it!" as Poppa laughed about "how good it feels to be saved, to know that the Lord Jesus Christ is my salvation and my redeemer!"

After church when the members would say, "Your poppa sho' did preach this morning," Joshua would blush and smile. "You gon' be jes' like him, ain't you?" and he would mumble "Yes'm" or "Yes, sir."

He would walk home with Poppa, his short legs stretching to match Poppa's long and easy stride, but the closer they came to home, the shorter Poppa's step became and by the time they walked through the gate, Poppa was almost shuffling and Joshua knew that come sundown, Poppa would put the bridle on one of the mules and slip into the night. He wished he knew why the Poppa of Sunday morning didn't tell the one of Sunday night to stop making friends with hellfire, and when summer was near dead, so did the church members.

It was late one Sunday afternoon when Brother Emory brought the word.

Joshua was sitting on the front porch step dreading the coming of night when he heard the gate swing open and saw Brother Emory step into the yard. He was a little man, the color of an autumn oak leaf, and everybody said he was old as autumn, too. He didn't look it. His knotty hair was white as a star, but his skin was smooth and he walked like he knew that the earth would hold him up. Poppa said that Brother Emory was born in slavery times. He never wore anything except bib overalls, sometimes with a brightly colored shirt underneath, as often not; sometimes he wore shoes; most times, he didn't. It was cool that afternoon and he had on a black-and-red-checked flannel shirt.

"How you this Sunday afternoon, Joshua?"

"Jus' fine, Brother Emory. How you?"

"Fair to middling," he responded, as Joshua had known he would. "Is the Reverend around?"

"Yes, sir. I'll get him for you."

But as Joshua got up to go in the house to get his father, the screen door opened and Poppa stepped out as sleek and black as a sinful thought.

"Brother Emory," Poppa said without smiling.

Joshua wanted to run away to the top of the hill back of the house, or through the cotton field, to run anywhere as fast and hard as he could, but he could not move.

"How you, Reverend?"

Poppa let the screen door close quietly behind him. "Come up and sit and take a load off your feet."

"Thank you, Reverend."

Poppa offered Brother Emory the straight-back chair and he sat down in the rocker.

"Go find something to do, boy," and the words freed Joshua, but instead of running away, he slipped quietly into the house and through the back door and around to the other side of the house where he crawled under the porch.

For a long time he heard nothing except the quiet back-and-forth motion of Poppa's rocking chair. It seemed like each was waiting for the other to speak first and each was daring the other to speak first and whoever did would lose.

But when Brother Emory finally spoke, he didn't sound like he'd lost anything.

"Charles, I been knowing you since before you knowed yourself. I knowed your daddy before you was a twinkle in his eye, and I remember ol' Tremble, your granddaddy, too. Didn't think too highly of him, though."

Joshua lay on his stomach in the dirt, eyes closed, barely breathing. He knew that when the old folks started off reciting your family history, they hadn't come to pass the time of day.

"You can skip all that, Brother Emory," he heard Poppa say roughly. "Get to the point."

There was another long silence, so long that Joshua began wondering if Brother Emory, old as autumn, had just vanished like the green in grass.

"And your granddaddy and daddy always had manners," Brother Emory finally said in a calm rebuke.

"You come here to give me a sermon about my folks?"

"Seems like somebody need to do some preaching to you."

Poppa laughed at that, but it wasn't the loving-God laugh, but more like sandpaper on an old, rough pine board that will never get smooth no matter how much you sand it.

"And who gon' preach to me? Every jook joint I go in,

13

I see you and some of the other brothers of the church. I know some of the members sent you over to talk to me. I ain't dumb. But who they think they is that they can talk to me?"

"That's just the point, Charles. Don't nobody have to tell me or any of the other members that we sinners. We know that. But you the preacher. And more than that, you one of us. Before you growed up and got the call, a preacher used to come here once a month, when the roads was passable. And no preacher would stay for more than a year or two. Who wants a little old country church way out here that can't pay nothing but loose change? But when you started preaching, we been having church every Sunday since. And you one of us. Everybody feel like a part of them in you."

"What you think I am? A patchwork quilt? I don't see what your point is. I is still the first one at church every Sunday and ain't never missed a Sunday. And, if I say so myself, I'm preaching better than I ever was."

"That's sho' 'nuf the truth. But there's more to preaching than preaching."

Poppa laughed loudly at that. "You ain't making no sense, Brother Emory."

Brother Emory continued as if Poppa hadn't spoken. "Like I said a minute ago, I know I'm a sinner, but I also got to know that it's possible not to be. And that's what the preacher is. I look at you, Charles, and hell, I feel like I'm better than you. And so does everybody else. You just saying the words up there on Sunday morning now. An old sinner like me might not act like I done heard the words or that I'm trying to live by'em, but you supposed to be the words and when I look at you, some of the words I may done forgot suppose to come back."

Joshua was sure Poppa was really going to be angry now,

but there was another silence as long as a sad night. Then he heard Poppa's voice break like a melody with notes missing.

"Ain't no God no more. What kind of God would take a man's chillun like He done mine? You answer me that!"

"Same God what let you sit here and breathe and talk about Him like that," Brother Emory said sharply. "You think you the only one whose babies done died? You got that little one that was here a minute ago. I had three in slavery what was all sold away. I had five since slavery. Three of'em is over there in the boneyard, one's on the chain gang, and the white folks killed the other one for something or other. What that got to do with God?"

Poppa's laugh was like winter. "Maybe you niggers ain't got the sense to see what I sees, and that's that there ain't no God, and if there is, might as well not be 'cause this One act like He don't give a damn."

Joshua heard the chair scrape on the porch floor, and he knew that it wasn't what Poppa said about God that made Brother Emory get up but that he'd called him a nigger.

"We don't want you for a preacher no more, Charles."

"You niggers don't want a preacher. You want a saint!"

Poppa was shouting now, but Brother Emory never said a word back and Joshua opened his eyes to see Brother Emory's bare feet, as old and gnarled as a slave's memory, walk past the house and out of the yard. Poppa gave a short, humpbacked laugh and then came a silence as deep as a wound.

Joshua didn't move from his hiding place until he heard Poppa stomp off the porch, until he saw the mule's hooves and Poppa's shiny black high-top shoes dangling from the mule's sides move past his low window on the world.

He crawled slowly out, brushed off his clothes, squinting against the late Sunday afternoon light. Then he went in the house and knocked softly on the door of his parents' room. There was no answer. He knocked again. Still getting no response, he turned the knob and entered quietly.

Momma was sitting in the rocker looking through the window past which Poppa had just ridden. She was as thin as a dream fragmenting on waking. Samuel, seated on her lap, must've been almost two then, and he looked at Joshua with ecclesiastical solemnity, then lay his head on her thin chest.

She didn't look at Joshua, nor turn her head when he sat on the side of her and Poppa's bed.

He sat, looking down at the dirt on his pants and shirt and waited for her to ask, "What's the matter, Joshua?," the way she used to when he was very quiet, to say, "How'd you get them clothes so dirty, boy? You must think I'm your personal washerwoman," to ask him to go out and pick some butter beans for supper, and if she had said or asked or even looked, he could've asked, "What's the matter with Poppa?"

She didn't, but just sat and stared out the window as if the future were staring balefully back while Samuel fell asleep on her lap and night came slowly, erasing her from Joshua's vision as if she were no more than a word written crudely on a slate board.

One evening the following week he bridled the best mule and rode into town. Even today, Ouichitta was still little more than a long block of stores facing each other on both sides of a street. Then, however, it was a short block with only the sheriff's office, jail, general store, blacksmith shop, and the white church. As he rode slowly up the street, four white men leaning against the hitching post in front of the general store stared at him with a calm antagonism. He continued to the end of the block and around the corner to the little café where the colored went to drink beer and moonshine, if Miz Tierny had paid off the high sheriff that month.

He stopped the mule at the hitching post but didn't get off.

"I'm looking for Dallas Smith," he said to the small crowd of sharecroppers and women loitering in front.

"Who wants to know?" someone asked finally.

"His brother."

A woman as yellow as churned butter, with a long ragged scar red as a sunset down one cheek, got off the bench in front of the café and walked to the hitching post. "You and him do kinna favor," she said in a voice rough as gravel.

She directed him to the Wellington plantation, which was two miles further out of town. At least that was where it began. He supposed all the land on both sides of the road, as far as he could see, was the Wellington plantation. The houses sat far back from the road, and with cotton plants growing to the front doors, the houses with their tin roofs looked more like overgrown and undernourished noxious weeds than places in which people lived.

He supposed it wouldn't take him long to find Dallas, since he was known to everybody after he killed Big Time. Joshua had overheard Poppa and Momma talking about it, but didn't know if it happened the day before, or before he was born. He'd been too young to understand the details, except that Dallas had killed somebody neither colored folks nor white folks liked and the high sheriff had told Dallas that it wouldn't be right to put him in jail for killing somebody like Big Time and that as long as he killed a nigger whose work the white folks wouldn't miss, he didn't give a damn how many niggers he killed.

So when Joshua rode up to a house where an old man and old woman sat on the porch, pipes in their teethless mouths, and asked for Dallas, they knew who he was and directed him further back into the plantation. "Jes' keep going, son. You'll hear the guitar."

He continued along the narrow path between the endless fields of cotton plants, whose bolls were beginning to open. The hot, still evening was interrupted only by the barking of a dog as the trail took him past another cabin. He could hear the distant sound of a bottleneck making the guitar string whine like all the world's sorrows.

It was dark when he saw the thin yellow light of kerosene lamps shining through the windows of a cabin at the edge of a stand of pine trees. He rode up to the house and tied the mule's reins to a porch support.

He stood in the darkness, his body recoiling from the loud laughter and shouting coming from within the cabin. Now that he was there, he didn't know what to do. He supposed he could go on the porch and look through the window, but Poppa had told him never to go to a jook joint. "That's what got your brother. Dallas been taken over by the devil women and devil water. He going straight to hell!"

Joshua patted the mule's rump, more to reassure himself than the mule, which stood quietly. Just then the sounds from inside got louder and he looked up to see the door opening and a woman stumble onto the porch, a jar of whiskey in her hand. She laughed loudly.

"Got to get some air, y'all. Soon as I catch my breath, I'll show you what dancing is, honey. You gon' get blue balls just from watching." She laughed again and lurched down the steps as the door closed behind her.

Joshua ducked beneath the mule to hide on the other side. He waited, and wondering what the woman was doing, edged toward the mule's rump and peered over to see her sitting on the bottom porch step.

In the dim light from the shack he saw that she had on a red dress that shone like light on glass. Her hair was long, wavy, and black, and a magnolia blossom was stuck behind one ear. Joshua swallowed hard. Was she a devil woman? But looking at her sitting there like she was all alone in the world, he thought she was the prettiest girl he'd ever seen or would ever see.

So intently was he staring that when the mule's tail suddenly swished at a mosquito, he was unprepared for the slap across his face and yelled, "Ouch!"

"Who's that?" the woman said, getting up quickly.

He slipped beneath the mule.

"Now, don't play games with me," the woman said. "Show yourself, nigger, or I'll get somebody out here to make you wish you had."

Joshua flattened himself on the ground beneath the mule, squeezing his eyes shut.

Suddenly he heard her laugh.

"Lawd, have mercy!" she exclaimed, laughing more.

He felt her hand on his shoulder and tried to move away, but she tightened her grip.

"Come here, honey. Earlene's not going to hurt you. Come on out from there before that mule gets you confused with the ground. You wouldn't want that to happen, would you?"

Her voice wasn't harsh and loud now.

"Come on, and let Earlene look at you. I think you might be kinna cute, but I can't tell with you trying to bury yourself in the ground. You be buried soon enough, chile. That's the God's truth!"

He let himself be coaxed out and, as he stood up, brushed at his pants and shirt.

"What's your name?"

"Joshua," he muttered, staring at the ground, hands clasped in front of him.

"Is you the one what fit' the battle of Jericho?" she asked, teasing.

"No'm," he responded, serious.

She laughed. "Lawd, I ain't never been called ma'am in my life. I'll sho' remember this moment as long as I live."

Joshua felt her hand beneath his chin and as she raised his head, he didn't resist. Her eyes were so big and warm, he knew she couldn't sin, even if she did have a jar of liquor in her hand. She smiled and he smiled back shyly.

"That's about the nicest smile Earlene has seen in a long time. You keep smiling at the girls like that, Joshua, and you'll break a lot of hearts."

She hugged him to her and his body stiffened at the soft slickness of her dress and the firm warmth beneath. He wanted to run and he wanted to let his cheek lie against her stomach, but she released him, took his hand, and led him to sit beside her on the porch step.

"What're you doing at a place like this? You kinna young to be hanging around a jook joint, ain't you? How old are you?"

"Nine," he lied.

"How come you not home in bed?"

"I come for my brother."

"What's his name?"

"Dallas."

Earlene looked at Joshua closely, then nodded. "What you want him for?"

"I need him to come home."

Earlene chuckled. "Joshua, I been knowing your brother a long time. I don't think there's no way you can convince him to do a thing 'cepting drink, play cards, shoot dice, and—well—and other things."

"He gotta! He gotta come home!" Joshua insisted. "He just gotta!"

"It's that serious?"

"Yes'm. Ain't nobody to take care of things but me. Poppa, Poppa ain't well. And Momma ain't neither."

She was silent for a minute. "You sit right here, baby."

She went inside and he waited, sitting on the bottom porch step and staring at the North Star. From inside there came suddenly the sound of the guitar crying sorrows only night could withstand and a man's voice as jagged and hard as broken glass:

"Nothing but blues and trouble
Standing in my way.
Nothing but blues and trouble
Standing in my way.
But when the sun come up,
Lord, it's gonna be another day."

"Sing it, T.J.!" Joshua heard someone shout.

"Lord, I'm going to Memphis
If I can find a train to ride.
Yes, I'm going to Memphis
If I can find a train to ride.
Said, I'm going to Memphis
And find someplace to hide."

Joshua shifted uneasily, wrapping his arms around his small body as if to protect himself from all the unknown sorrows, past and still to be known. Why had he bothered to come? Dallas would just laugh and tell him to go home.

He had been four when Dallas left. All he remembered was standing on the porch with Momma, and she was screaming and Myra and Sue Ann were crying and he was leaning against Momma's trembling legs and holding tightly to her dress. Poppa lay on the ground in the front yard curled up like a baby and holding his stomach, puke coming out of his mouth and Dallas stood over him, his fists clenched, yelling, "Git up, goddammit! Git up!" But Poppa didn't, and when Dallas knew finally that he wouldn't, his fists opened and he walked slowly to the porch and hugged Momma and Myra and Sue Ann good-bye and when he stooped to hug Joshua, Joshua ran to where Poppa lay on the ground and tried to put his arm around Poppa's trembling shoulders.

Dallas would come back several times a year to see Momma. Poppa would leave the house, taking Joshua with him.

"You ain't gon' put the devil in this boy! Not if I got any say in the matter. Joshua ain't gon' be the devil's henchman. He's gonna be a righteous man!"

Dallas would laugh as if he'd just been told a dirty secret.

The music and noise from inside was louder as the door opened, and Joshua turned quickly, but it wasn't Earlene and it wasn't his brother, but the shadowy form of a man who lurched down the steps and to the edge of the yard where he put a finger down his throat, gagged, and vomited. Joshua pinched his nose against the stench of regurgitated rotgut whiskey. The man vomited again, belched loudly, sighed. He wiped his mouth on the sleeve of his shirt, giggled, and staggered back into the house without a glance at Joshua.

When Dallas came out finally, Joshua was asleep.

"Well, well, well. If it ain't the little preacher. What you want?"

Joshua rubbed his eyes and looked up at the big man ten years older than him, the man Momma said was his brother, no matter how Poppa felt. Dallas was tall like their father, but bigger and broader. He wore a black cowboy hat tilted back on his head, and his black shirt was half unbuttoned, and in the light of the match Dallas struck with his thumbnail to light a cigarette, Joshua could see little knots of kinky hair on his chest.

"You gotta come home," Joshua said earnestly, standing up.

"And why I *gotta* come home?" Dallas asked harshly. "Poppa need a hand to pick cotton? Is that it? Well, if it is, Poppa know I done picked my last boll of cotton, last pole bean, and last ear of corn. I don't plan on seeing no more cotton unless'n it's been made into a shirt." He laughed.

"I don't know nothing about that," Joshua rushed on. "Poppa didn't send me and Momma don't know I come. Ain't nothing been the same since Sue Ann died."

"Sue Ann dead?" Dallas asked, his voice shocked, losing its harshness for the first time.

"Ain't nobody now 'cepting me and the baby. Momma, she just sit and stare. And Poppa, well, Poppa. . . ." He stopped.

"Poppa what?" Dallas asked quickly, his voice a tangle of eagerness and fear.

"He drinking a lot and never at home," Joshua answered, scarcely audible.

Dallas laughed loudly with a mad glee. "You don't say! Well, I'll be goddammed. Poppa finally seen the error of his ways, huh?"

"You gotta come home, Dallas. You just gotta," his voice rising and tightening until it sounded like a broken bottle-neck on a guitar string.

The big man stared down at the little boy. "You go on back," he said finally. "I be there."

Dallas came the next day before sundown and Joshua wished he could've made his mother smile by walking in the house like he'd just bought it. Poppa came home the night after and was almost on the porch before he saw Dallas sitting in his rocker. He stopped, but didn't say anything. He just stood and stared and Dallas rocked and stared, and it was like a contest to see who was going to look away first, or speak first, or move first, or bat his eyes first, though

Joshua couldn't see their eyes in the dark, but he did see when Poppa lowered his head and walked on the porch, past Dallas, and into the house. Joshua didn't know if Poppa heard Dallas's low chuckle. Joshua thought he heard his father's footsteps on the porch just before false dawn, but he fell back to sleep before he could get up to see. When he got up at daybreak, though, Poppa was gone.

Even now, sitting at his desk, head bowed as if he had fallen into death, even now, seeing, even now, his father, even, now, was flesh and substance, remembered in his own dying body as something tangible which he'd misplaced and would find one day in the obvious place he'd been sure it wasn't, tall, lanky, black as midnight in hell, a black felt cowboy hat on his head, looking as if he could challenge heaven's dominion—that was how he remembered him, and Reverend Smith smiled, though the corners of his mouth did not turn upward.

It wasn't easy in that time and place for a black man to own forty acres of prime land. Wasn't no other colored in Ouichitta County owned that much land. Most had to work on the Wellington plantation, where they didn't own their lives.

During the year between the deaths of Myra and Sue Ann, Poppa took Joshua in the wagon and drove up the hill behind the house, slapping the mule on the rump with the reins when the road ended at the corral on the crest. The mule balked at continuing across the field of weeds, grasses, and wild flowers, but Poppa hollered "Giddap!" and the mule moved with stubborn slowness along the ridge.

This was the highest point on the forty acres and Joshua liked to come there sometimes and look across to the next ridge, wondering if someone stood there looking toward him, wondering.

"Whoa!" his father called gently, pulling back on the

reins, though the mule had almost slowed to a halt on its own.

Joshua leaped down and ran after his father, who was already walking across the ridge with long, sure strides. The sun was high in the clear sky but not hot as it would be in another week or so. The trees fluttered with new green reminding Joshua of another April day when he came to the ridge and while running through the high grass stopped suddenly at a sound like sand shaken in a paper sack. He had never heard the sound before, but his body stopped, as if turned to stone. He waited until the sound came again, soft, menacing, stilling even nature as not a leaf fluttered or bird sang. He located the sound six feet in front of him and to the left. As quietly as a blade of grass growing through the earth, he backed away.

When his father stopped suddenly, Joshua wondered if he'd heard a rattler, too. Poppa was staring down the hill at the grove of trees which formed the southern boundary of the property, trees which Poppa said were never to be cut. Joshua looked up at his father, wondering what he was listening to, or wanted to see.

"Come on," Poppa said brusquely, starting down the hill. Joshua ran beside him, jumping and galloping through the high grass, not caring now where his father was going or why, not listening for the sound of sand in a paper bag, not caring if he stepped on a rattler as big around as the oak tree in Ouichitta where Tommy Dyer was hung last year, because he was with Poppa where fear could not be.

"There it is yonder," Poppa said, pointing.

"What?"

Poppa stopped and Joshua followed the invisible line from his father's extended forefinger. He squinted and still saw nothing.

"Look close now."

Joshua squinted even more, furrowing his brow, his eyes slits and everything blurred and there, amidst the tall grasses near the bottom of the hill he thought he saw rusted iron spires sticking out of the earth.

"Come on."

As they came closer Joshua saw a wrought-iron fence making a perfect square inside of which two rows of small tombstones seemed to have grown like petrified flowers.

Poppa was walking slowly now, almost reverentially, and Joshua wondered why people's bodies became quiet around the dead.

"I come up here when I knowed Myra was going to die and I cleaned it out real good. Pulled all the weeds and cut it good," he announced with rough pride.

Joshua followed his father through an opening in the fence where the gate would have been. Poppa stopped and stared at the six tombstones in two rows of three. Joshua's hand found his father's and held it tightly. His body was quiet now, too. The tombstones were not bright and shiny like the ones in the white cemetery in town. These were slabs of stone, rounded at the top. Writing was carved on the faces, but the repetition of rain and sun and cold had worn the soft stone until the lettering was indecipherable. A corner of one stone had broken and lay crumbling on the ground.

"I wanted to bury Myra here, but I hadn't put none of the rest of my children up here. So I decided to put her in the colored cemetery with Pecola, Alice, and Pauline. That way she won't be forgot. Other peoples coming to the cemetery over the years will see her name on the stone and read it to theyselves. Bury her up here and she be forgot pretty quick, just like these here been forgot."

Joshua didn't think Poppa was talking to him, because his voice had the sound of a thought that came in the night.

Poppa loosened his hand from Joshua's and knelt for a moment before each tombstone, his eyes closed. Whatever prayer he prayed was between him and God, because Joshua heard nothing except a robin somewhere on the ridge and crows in the grove of trees at the bottom of the hill.

"Them's your grands," Poppa said when he finished. "That one at the far end of this first row was the first and the one next to him is your great-grandma. The one next to her is their oldest girl. She was the only one what stayed in Ouichitta. Others went off somewheres or other and ain't nobody heard from them since. Them three on the second row is my poppa and momma and my only sister. When the time come, you lay me side of her. You understand?"

"Yes, suh," Joshua said solemnly.

They left the cemetery and as they began the slow walk back up the hill, Poppa told his second son about the man named Tremble Smith, "the first one's grave I showed you. That was sho' 'nuf his name. Back in slavery times the colored had all kinds of funny-sounding names. Caesar. Pompey. Least they sound funny to us now. Must've sounded just fine to them, I reckon. All this land what I showed you today wouldn't be ours if it hadn't been for Tremble.

"The way it was handed to me, it went like this: Tremble was a slave on the Wellington plantation. They the ancestors of the Wellingtons what run it now. Tremble wasn't no ordinary kind of slave. Uh-uh. Even if he was a slave, he had more sense than a lot of these niggers walking around here today who have to beg the white man for every crumb.

"Tremble knowed he was a slave, but he also knowed he was a man. That's the difference between him and these niggers like your brother, Dallas, who 'fraid to be men. And back in slavery times, way I hear tell it, you had to keep your knowledge of being a man to yourself if you didn't want to get killed. Tremble Smith had a lot of sense. He didn't have no book learning at that time, but there's only one kind of sense in them books. The best sense you can learn is to watch people. You listenin' to me?"

"Yes, suh," Joshua responded promptly.

"That's good," his father continued, his breath and words coming with effort as the slope steepened. "I'm telling you what I know, not what I think. Now, like I was saying, Tremble was a man, wanted to live like a man, but didn't know how he could, being in slavery like he was. So he waited and watched and one day his time come.

"Now, Tremble wasn't one of them slaves that worked in the field hoeing and picking cotton. He was what you call a many-sided man. He could build a house as good as any anywhere. Built a white lady a house there in Ouichitta with five fireplaces that all drew through one flue. He could pick the guitar and make that box do everything except add and subtract figures. His massa said he was too valuable to be working in the fields, so he had Tremble do all the carpentry work on the plantation. Every now and then he'd loan him out to other plantation owners when they needed a chest or table or something like that built. Tremble and Josie, his wife, lived right there in the big house, 'cause she was the lady servant for the ol' missus.

"But as much as Tremble was around the white folks, he made sure to keep the friendship of the slaves what worked in the fields. He built all their houses and fixed 'em up when they was leaking and what not. He wasn't like the other house servants who thought they was better than them what worked in the field.

"Now, the way it happened was like this: One evening Tremble was down in the slave quarters fixing somethin' for somebody and a slave took him off to the side and told him that they was planning an uprising and were going to kill all the white folks. Said that since Tremble had always been nice to them and 'cause Josie would slip food from the massa's table to'em when she could, they wanted him and Josie to be spared. Said they was going to kill the other house niggers with pleasure, but it wouldn't pleasure nobody to kill him and Josie.''

Poppa stopped and sat down in the grass. Joshua sat next to him, staring down the slope where he could see the iron spires clearly, now that he knew where to look.

Poppa chuckled. ''Your great-granddaddy was a thinking man, and he done some fast thinking that night. He asked the slave when the uprising was to be. The slave said they was going to move on the full moon, 'cause they could see better how to get around. Tremble told him they could also be seen better. Said that owls and all the night birds get spooky when the moon is full. Slave said they hadn't thought of that. Tremble went on and said that the big house was locked up tight at night and if the slaves was smart, they'd let him unlock the door for'em, and furthermore, he'd draw a map of the house and that way they could move on the dark of the moon.

''Well, the slave was happy with what Tremble had to say. Said he never thought Tremble would want to join up with'em. So Tremble drawed a diagram of the house in the dust, showing where every room was, all the stairs, even telling him which steps on the stairway creaked.''

Poppa stopped talking and Joshua turned to look at him. His father was staring down the slope again and when he spoke, his voice was hesitant, weak, almost fearful.

''A lot of folks might not approve of what Tremble done next. Fact is, *I know* most folks wouldn't. I done thought about it a lot and I say you can't criticize a man if you ain't never tried to fit in his britches. I don't know if what Tremble done was right or wrong, and God knows I wish I did.

My mind would rest easy if I knowed for sure it was right. But I'm just telling you like I heard it from Poppa, who got the story from Tremble.

"Now, the massa used to let Tremble come and go pretty much as he wanted, because he had to roam around the countryside to find the right trees suitable for whatever needed building. Tremble would take a mule and wagon from the barn, a maul, and some saws and go out to get his trees, and during his many trips like that, he found this land right here and fell in love with it.

"So one afternoon a few days after the slave had spoke with him, he asked the master to come and inspect some trees. They come out here in the wagon, and as they was riding past, Tremble said, 'Massa, that's mighty good land you got from here all the way back of that ridge yonder.'

"Massa allowed as how it was.

" 'A man could make a good living just from selling the timber, and if he planted cotton down here in the valley, he'd do mighty well. Ain't that so, massa?'

"Massa allowed as to how that was true, too, but that it would take too many slaves to work all that land. He said he was planning to give the land to his children one day.

"Tremble said, 'I wouldn't do that if I was you. I want that land.' "

Poppa laughed loudly, slapping his thighs. "Son, don't you know that white man got so mad that his face turned all red like white folks' faces do. But Tremble act like he don't notice. Just kept the mule moving real slow.

" 'Giving me that forty acres is better than being dead, massa.'

"Well, Tremble got the massa's attention sho' 'nuf now, and the massa wanted to know if Tremble was threatening to kill him. He say he know Tremble ain't gon' crazy, so what the dickens was he talking about? That wasn't exactly what he said, but you understand."

Joshua grinned and nodded.

"Now, this is where Tremble showed how smart he was. He didn't tell his master what he meant. That made massa more mad and he threatened to beat it out of Tremble.

"Tremble told him he'd never find out then. Well, what could massa do? He knew that Tremble was on to something big, because Tremble wasn't like some niggers what just make up stuff to tell the white folks to try and get in their favor.

"So he asked Tremble what he wanted. Tremble told him to draw up a deed for the land and write it all out legal. Massa didn't want to do that, but what choice did he have?"

Poppa chuckled. "But Tremble wasn't through. He had sense enough to know that a slave couldn't own land, and he knowed that massa knowed it, too. So a couple of days later when massa called Tremble in his study and give him the deed to the land, Tremble told him the deed wasn't no good without freedom papers for him and Josie. Well, massa like to have an apopleptic fit sho' 'nuf this time, but after he got through cussing and threatening, he wrote the papers out and give'em to Tremble. Tremble took his time and read through the papers, which give ol' massa another shock, 'cause he didn't know Tremble could read. When Tremble was satisfied that the papers said what he wanted'em to say, he told massa about the uprising, when it was going to take place and who was in it."

He stopped and Joshua looked up to see a face pinched with sorrow and confusion.

"I don't understand it myself," he said finally, shaking his head. "A lot of folks would say he was a traitor to his people for doing something like that. And I suppose there ain't no way around that. He was. But that ain't the way Tremble seen it, not if I understood what my poppa told me.

31

"If you think real hard on it," he continued, his voice strong with urgency now, as if he had to convince Joshua, "what do you think would've happened if Tremble hadn't told? Suppose the slaves had risen up like they was planning. Well, you young, but you done lived on this earth long enough to see how white mens treat us colored. Like that boy they lynched in Ouichitta last year. They cut off his privates like he was a stallion and put'em in a big jar of alcohol and kept it in the window of the general store until right before Christmas. If they do us like that now, they done worse back in slavery times.

"Now, to begin with, the uprising didn't stand a chance. The slaves had axes and hoes and shovels. Massa had guns. Let's say, however, that the slaves had managed to kill massa, his wife, and chillun. Don't you know that as soon as the white folks on the neighboring plantations learned of it, they would have come with their guns and killed every nigger on the plantation, whether he had a part of the thing or not. Not only that, but niggers all over this part of Mississippi would have suffered something terrible, like they did after that boy got lynched last year. You remember?"

Joshua nodded, remembering how the Kluxers had gone into houses and beat everybody with whips.

"Miz Patterson's boy, Lee, got beat up so bad that he's paralyzed to this day. And he hadn't done nothing to nobody.

"Tremble said he saved a lot of slaves from getting killed, ones who didn't even know an uprising was planned." Poppa shook his head. "I don't know the truth of the matter. I just know the facts and that's what I give you. Someday you'll be smarter than me and maybe you can figure it out for me."

He looked down at Joshua and smiled, hugging the boy

to him. "Guess it's time we was getting on back.

"I don't know if you understand what I'm trying to tell you," he continued seriously as they started up the hill again. "There's parts of the story I don't understand, but this much I do. There ain't no way that a colored man can be a man in this white man's world if he don't understand that he has to use whatever power he can get. You hear me? If Tremble Smith hadn't known that, we'd be living on the Wellington plantation right now working on shares and getting deeper in debt. All this land I showed you today has been ours since 1827. That was deep back in slavery time. But Tremble got it and held on to it, and maybe sometime I'll tell you all the things the white folks done to try and get it from him. If I knowed what that man knowed, I'd own the whole state of Mississippi." He chuckled. When he resumed, his voice was wistful. "I reckon I know, but knowing and doing, well, Tremble had the heart for the doing."

Reverend Smith blinked his eyes, and the green blotter, the papers and envelopes and file folders on it came into focus. Was it possible for an eighty-year-old man to miss his father as if he were still a boy sitting on a hillside in the afternoon of a spring day being taught what he needed to know?

He blinked his eyes and a tear trailed down his face. Moments without thought passed before he raised a trembling hand and, pressing it to his cheek, dragged it clumsily down his face to wipe away the tear.

He liked the little boy into whose keeping the family had been passed that afternoon. He even liked the little boy who sat behind the large desk, the salty taste of dried tears in the corner of his mouth. Except ye be as little children, Jesus had said. He didn't say be little children, however.

33

Reverend Smith had preached about that many times, and if it had not been too much effort, if he could've remembered exactly where to look, he would've taken the sermon from the filing cabinet to read.

Except ye be as a little child even as he was an old and weary man waiting for death as eagerly as he had waited for Poppa to drive up the road from town on Saturdays. That was before Sue Ann died.

After Dallas came back, Poppa came home only when someone brought him in the back of a buckboard. Sometimes Momma got up and helped him into the house and sometimes, Dallas did. After a while, people stopped bringing him and he didn't come.

Reverend Smith had never told Josh or Carl about their grandfather's drinking. "Your granddaddy was a preacher," was all he'd ever told them, and, he didn't know why he would die without saying more about him.

Was it because there would be too much to tell, or that there was nothing? Or, was it that it was hard to tell what couldn't be understood just by listening, and if that was the way of it, would anybody be better off for the telling?

He remembered lying half asleep in bed during that first month after Dallas came, unable to sleep because of the monstrous noises come from where Dallas slept on the bed that had been put in the corner of the room, unable to sleep because he was listening for the sound of a wagon's wheels, or of Poppa stumbling onto the porch. A month passed with the night giving back no sound except of itself.

Late one afternoon, he rode a mule to town and there Poppa was, sitting on a bench in front of Miz Tierny's place, his back against the storefront, his head over on his shoulder like he'd been lynched.

After that it was like a game of hide-and-seek, and when Joshua would eventually find him in a jook joint hidden among pine trees high on a mountain ridge, or in some lady's shack on the Wellington plantation, Poppa would chuckle with delight.

"Made you do some sho'-'nuf hunting this time, didn't I?"

Joshua didn't see the fun in it. He wouldn't say anything, but would help Poppa onto the mule and then jump on himself, Poppa's arms hooked loosely around his waist, and they would go home. Poppa would stay a day or two, maybe a week. He and Dallas would talk about the weather at supper, and then Dallas and Momma would start talking and laughing about when Dallas was a baby, or the time she took him and Pecola to Memphis to visit her sister, and Joshua would try hard to think of something he could talk to Poppa about while Poppa ate faster and faster and was gone from the table while Joshua was still scurrying through memory like a squirrel looking for the hidden morsel that would make the winter bearable. He could never find it and always, he would awaken one morning and, without opening his eyes, know that Poppa had left in the night.

On one of those times he'd brought him home, Poppa got Momma pregnant. Joshua was ten when Louis was born and he remembered sitting on the front porch with Sister Winston, the midwife, and Dallas, who were both angry and tired from his mother's long labor.

"He ought to be shot," Sister Winston said, sticking her stubby pipe in her mouth and lighting it. "Mary needed to birth another baby like I need poison. Her body is so wore out from birthing babies that it's like a piece of land that ain't no good because wasn't nothing growed in it but cotton."

"He got no right bringing more chillun into the world that he ain't gon' support," Dallas added. "I'm more daddy to his chillun than he is."

"That's so," Sister Winston agreed, "though I suspecks don't nobody show you no appreciation for it."

Joshua was sitting on the porch step and he turned to look at Sister Winston, his face burning, and she was glaring at him, as if he had made Momma pregnant.

Sammy thought Dallas was his poppa, because he didn't know nobody else for a poppa. But Joshua could remember before and maybe he bridled the mule and hunted for Poppa every time the moon was in the sky like a communion wafer because he didn't want to forget.

Sometimes when he'd find Poppa in a jook joint, or sitting at a rickety table eating supper at some lady's house, Poppa would smile at him, and it was like nothing had happened, even though Poppa's clothes were wrinkled and dirty, and his shoes were laced with pieces of wrapping string, and the whiskey smell was in his sweat.

Poppa would smile and tell his lady friend to get another plate. "This here is my son," he would announce with pride.

Joshua would smile and sit at the table next to his father and eat the pig feet and white beans, or a mess of greens with a little piece of ham in them. And when they finished eating, Poppa would chuckle, "Well, I guess we better hit the road, Joshua."

He liked it best at times like that when Poppa was sober and he rode behind Poppa on the mule, his arms hugging his father's waist tightly as the mule plodded along the road, and for as long as it took them to get home, everything was like it was supposed to be.

If it didn't stay that way, it was enough knowing that once in a while, it could be how it used to be and if Poppa forgot, Joshua would just have to remember for both of them.

It happened the winter after he turned fourteen. Six years had passed since sorrow, like shoats at the teats of a sow, had come to Poppa and Joshua had had to get Dallas to come back. Joshua didn't have to bend his head back so far now to look in Dallas's face, a face that regarded him as little more than a hand he didn't have to pay wages. Momma was better and she'd done more canning that fall than she had since Myra died—pears, apple butter, enough tomatoes to feed Ouichitta County, green beans, peas, carrots, mustard, turnip and collard greens. And in the evenings Joshua could hear Momma and Dallas laughing and talking in her and Poppa's room while he got Samuel and Louis ready for bed.

That Sunday morning of his fourteenth winter, Joshua had gotten up early to fix breakfast for Louis and Samuel. He had stopped asking his mother to go to church with him, and Dallas had finally stopped telling him that he was wasting good sleeping time with a bunch of hypocrites without whom every jook joint in Ouichitta would go out of business.

It was cold when he left the barn to walk the two miles to church. The hills of northern Mississippi were brown, the trees bare against a sky as gray as a washtub and flat like a broad straight road. He'd planned to ride one of the mules, but Dallas had told him he couldn't, though he'd said nothing the Sunday before when Joshua had bridled and ridden the mule to church. This Sunday all he said was that Sunday was a day of rest and that's what he and the mule were going to do.

Evil. That's what Dallas was. He seemed to enjoy it like somebody drinking a cold drink of soda pop on a hot day. There were mornings when Joshua would be harnessing the mule for plowing and would look around to see Dallas standing just inside the barn door staring at him, a toothpick in the corner of his mouth, his cowboy hat set back on his head.

"Something the matter?" Joshua would want to know.

"Don't look like it to me."

"Then what you looking at?"

"Jus' nothing." He'd chuckle and stroll away.

Some nights as Joshua sat at the kitchen table studying by the light of the kerosene lamp, Dallas sat opposite, the newspaper flat on the table in front of him. But whenever Joshua looked up, his eyes were met by the hateful stare of his older brother.

"Something wrong?"

"You."

One night Dallas interrupted Joshua's studying to ask in a harsh voice, "What you see in them books?"

"We got to know as much as the white man know if we going to get ahead as a people," he responded primly.

Dallas grunted. "What fool told you that?"

"That's what 'Fessa Williamson say."

"And once you know much as the white man know, then what?"

Joshua's eyes wandered back to the book lying flat on the table. He shrugged. "I dunno," he answered weakly.

"You think the white man gon' gi' you his job once you know much as he do? Or let you marry his daughter? He gon' let you vote? He gon' call you 'suh' instead of 'boy'? Maybe you think he gon' shine your shoes and wait on you? That what you think?"

Joshua stared at the printed page wishing he could hide amidst its letters. "Maybe. Someday," he said unconvincingly.

Dallas laughed. "Nigger, if you think that, you better stop studying in them books so much, 'cause studying makin' you dumber than you already was."

There was another night, though.

"What that say?" Dallas demanded, shoving the newspaper across the table to Joshua.

"What you ask me for? You can read," Joshua answered, not moving to take the newspaper.

"You sassin' me, boy? Poppa might think you too good to lay a hand on, but he's laying over there in the bedroom sleepin' it off. You sass me and I'll make you wish you hadn't been born."

"What you want me to read?" Joshua asked after a deliberate pause.

"What it say there on the front page about cotton?"

Joshua took the paper and began reading aloud rapidly.

"Slow down, boy! Read so somebody can understand the words."

Joshua read more slowly, and when he finished, Dallas grunted and took back the paper. Every night thereafter, he asked Joshua to read more and more of the paper to him, and one evening as Joshua walked toward the kitchen with his books, he saw Dallas sitting at the table, his index finger pressed against the face of the paper, body hunched over it, lips moving as slowly as winter. Joshua turned around and went quietly back to the front of the house and lay down on the bed he shared with Samuel and Louis, who were already asleep.

He didn't argue that morning when Dallas told him he couldn't ride the mule. He merely nodded and started along the path across the yard and through the trees to the road.

The road was empty as it always was on Sunday morning. He liked to be the first to arrive at church. In the summer it gave him time to go behind the unpainted frame building and wipe the dust from his shoes with his spare handkerchief, straighten his tie, and knock the dust from his suit.

He wouldn't have to do that this morning. The hoof marks of mules and horses and the ruts of wagon wheels were frozen into the road and he walked with his head down to keep from tripping over the hard clods of earth.

Despite the cold he didn't mind the walk. It was as if church had already begun, because he was away from Dallas and Poppa. There was something different about church-going people. They didn't call each other nigger, or black son of a bitch, but Brother and Sister, as if everybody who let God into their hearts had the same parent who was God the Father.

They dressed in somber, dark clothes, clean and well pressed. He felt pure and real when he was with them. Not that he wasn't real when he slopped the hogs, plowed, weeded, or picked in the fields, or cut wood for the winter and stacked it next to the house. That was real, too, but not real like when he sat on the rough bench in church on Sunday morning and sang, "Holy, holy, holy, Lord God Almighty."

When he arrived at church, he went to the woodpile in the back and carried kindling and two logs inside to start a fire in the potbellied stove in the center of the small room. There wouldn't be many coming that morning. The preacher had been there last Sunday and only the truly faithful came the other three Sundays. He hadn't been saved yet, but he liked to think of himself as one of the faithful.

As the kindling caught fire and ignited the small logs, Joshua carried in more wood, filling the woodbox beside the back door, taking only one log in each hand so as not to dirty his overcoat. When the woodbox was filled, he put more logs on the now-blazing fire and stood close to the stove to warm his chilled body.

Time passed and no one came, not even Brother Emory who never missed. Joshua took the gold-plated watch from his pants pocket, the one Poppa wore before Joshua sneaked it from his pocket, afraid his father would exchange it for a bottle one night, or get it stolen. Poppa had never missed it.

Joshua stared at the watch and dropped it back in his pocket. No one was coming. Not that late. He left the warmth of the stove, went to the front door, and looked up and down the road. It was empty. He stood there a moment longer and then went back inside.

He supposed he should go home, but God would be so alone if he didn't say a prayer or read a passage of scripture, at least.

Joshua walked nervously to the pulpit and opened the large Bible. He turned the pages aimlessly, not knowing what he was looking for and suddenly unable to recall a single verse of the hundreds he'd memorized.

He found himself staring at the opening words of the Twenty-seventh Psalm and without knowing why, or even how, he heard his voice in his ears:

"The Lord is my light and my salvation; whom shall I fear? the Lord is the strength of my life; of whom shall I be afraid?"

The voice was young and it pronounced the words slowly as if the voice of the psalmist were speaking what had never been uttered until that moment.

"When the wicked, even mine enemies and my foes, came upon me to eat up my flesh, they stumbled and fell. Though an host should encamp against me, my heart shall not fear: though war should rise against me, in this will I be confident.

"One thing have I desired of the Lord, that will I seek after; that I may dwell in the house of the Lord all the days of my life, to behold the beauty of the Lord, and to enquire in his temple."

The voice was deeper and fuller now, as if the breath he saw on the still and chill air of the church was also being warmed, filling cavities within him.

"For in the time of trouble he shall hide me in his pavilion: in the secret of his tabernacle shall he hide me; he shall set me up upon a rock.

"And now shall mine head be lifted up above mine enemies round about me: therefore will I offer in his tabernacle sacrifices of joy; I will sing, yea, I will sing praises unto the Lord."

Joshua did not see the empty, handmade benches in front of him, nor the day as drab and flat as a cooling board, but only the sun and this world as flat and gray as the sky.

"Hear, O Lord, when I cry with my voice: have mercy also upon me, and answer me.

"When thou saidst, Seek ye my face; my heart said unto thee, Thy face, Lord, will I seek.

"Hide not thy face far from me; put not thy servant away in anger: thou hast been my help; leave me not, neither forsake me, O God of my salvation.

"When my father and my mother forsake me, then the Lord will take me up."

And he was raised into the air, spinning, whirling, and down below was the church and the road hard with cold and the bare and brown hills before everything became gray as he tumbled up through the layer of clouds, faster and faster and spilling over him, warm and wet and red as strawberries and blood, the sweet thick cooling Blood of the Lamb of God and it came from above and below and from every side until there was only the Blood of the Lamb of God and him within undulating like a weed on the sandy bottom of a river and he was taken higher and higher and faster and faster and he looked up to see stars above his head and he looked before him to see white-robed Jesus a lamb in his arms and Joshua ran to Jesus who held out one arm, cradling the lamb in the other and Joshua laughed and cried on the bosom of Jesus who cradled him as if he were a lamb and then Joshua was whirled and spun even higher and he looked down and the stars were beneath his feet but light was all around and the higher he was taken the brighter was the light and Joshua closed his eyes against it and the light burned his face and hands and as he raised his arms to protect himself from the light, all was suddenly still and silence covered him like an endless sea.

"Thank you, Father," he whispered and like blood pouring from a wound, tears poured from him as if his body cried.

"Thank you, Father," he whispered again and again and he did not notice the gray sky darkening outside. He did not notice the chill in the church harden into cold.

He was on fire from the light of God.

He ran out of the church and down the road, ran the two miles home, shouting, "I been saved! I been saved!"

Reverend Smith supposed that if anybody did something like that now they'd be put in the crazy house. When he was a boy, however, folks took religion seriously. They knew that nothing mattered in this life except whether your feet were on the Heaven-bound road or the one to Hell.

Wasn't many who believed that anymore. Oh, he knew that the churches were filled every Sunday, but people nowadays thought religion was supposed to be easy. They didn't know that when God laid his hands on you that you were marked with a burning brand. God told Abraham to sacrifice his son, and told His own son to die on a cross between two common thieves.

"Wait, I say, on the Lord," Reverend Smith said aloud, quoting the last words of the psalm he had read that morning in the empty church. "Wait, I say, on the Lord!" he repeated emphatically.

Folks didn't know how to wait. They thought it meant standing in a line at the supermarket. That wasn't it at all. The Bible said, "Wait on the Lord," not "wait for." Wait

on meant to serve the Lord, do His will, do what He beckoned, and come when He called.

Reverend Smith smiled to himself. He could still *think*
a better sermon than most preachers could preach. But that
was because men now got their religion in a seminary. They
didn't cry out and feel God's fire twisting through their
innards like a hot wire. They were too educated to run
down the road, yelling, "I been saved! Praise the Lord! I
been saved!"

The next year, on New Year's morning, Joshua was going
to the barn to feed the mules when the high sheriff drove
in the yard, his two fine horses pulling a buckboard. Poppa
lay in it, dead. The sheriff had found him lying in a ditch,
frozen.

Momma died a year later and Dallas took all the money
from the cotton crop and left. Joshua was sixteen. Sammy
was ten. Louis was six.

Reverend Smith knew he couldn't have survived without
waiting on the Lord. Poppa one year. Momma the next.
Left alone in the house with no money and two little boys.
They used all the canned vegetables quickly. Joshua killed
most of the chickens, leaving only enough for laying eggs.
Sometimes early on Saturday mornings he took the rifle and
hunted rabbit or squirrel. As tasty as squirrel was, squirrels
were more tail than meat.

He would never forget the cold February morning when
he stoked the fire in the potbellied stove, put in a load of
logs, and got Sammy and Louis up.

He made cornmeal cakes, not telling them he was using
the last of the flour and meal. He set the cornmeal cakes
and a jar of syrup on the table and told them to eat.

"Ain't you gon' eat?" Louis wanted to know.

"I'm not hungry," he lied.

Saying good-bye to the boys sitting at the table sopping

their cakes in the dark syrup, Joshua went to the barn, harnessed a mule to the wagon, and set off for town.

He sat hunched on the wagon seat against the cold as the wagon rumbled and lurched over the hard, frozen ruts. He kept one hand and then the other in his pocket, but his hands were quickly as knotted with cold as the road.

As the mule pulled the wagon closer and closer to town, he wondered if he was the only person left in the world. No one walked along the road; no wagons approached coming from town and looking behind, no wagons followed his. Every house was shut tight as if the inhabitants had slipped away in the night, leaving thin streams of smoke to rise from the chimneys like mourning ghosts trailing shrouds to spread over heaven. Occasionally a crow flew overhead, flapping its great black wings slowly as it seemed to come from nowhere.

Nothing moved except the mule pulling the wagon with a sixteen-year-old boy seated on it, his body drawn tight against the cold.

"Oh, Lord," he prayed, "I put myself in Your hands. Without You I am no better than a crow, going nowhere. Without You I am alone, no more than smoke rising through the chimney and disappearing in the air. You know my situation. I put myself in Your hands, Father. Amen."

His body relaxed and he sat up straighter. He liked talking to God better than anything in the world. Before he went to sleep each night, he knelt beside the bed and prayed, and sometimes awoke the next morning to find that he'd fallen asleep on his knees. He told God everything— about not burying Poppa on the hillside and feeling guilty for thinking that Poppa didn't deserve to be buried there, about Momma not wanting to live and how she sat in her room rocking back and forth and when he brought her supper she called him Charles and tried to kiss him like she had Poppa. Mostly when Joshua prayed, however, he told God how much he loved Him. Sometimes he just quoted verses from psalms he'd memorized.

"I love the Lord, because He hath heard my voice and my supplications. Because He hath inclined His ear unto me, therefore will I call upon Him as long as I live.

"Praise ye the Lord: for it is good to sing praises unto our God; for it is pleasant; and praise is comely."

A smile opened across his face, and he said:

"While I live will I praise the Lord. I will sing praises unto my God while I have any being."

He laughed, and if he hadn't been close to town, he would've shouted, "Praise the Lord! Praise His glorious name!" Instead he laughed again, slapped the mule with the reins, and the mule quickened its pace as the road became smoother.

As Joshua stopped in front of the general store, he noticed that Ouichitta's single street was empty, too. He got down from the wagon and tied the mule to the railing, nervous and afraid again, not knowing what to say or who to say it to. He'd never worked for white people. Nobody in his family had since Tremble got out of slavery.

Blowing on his hands, he walked into the general store. It was warm inside and Joshua went directly to the stove in the center of the room. He'd been in the store many times, because Poppa had bought seed and guano there, and Momma had bought bolts of cloth to make their clothes.

"Mawnin' Mistah Ralph, suh," Joshua greeted the white man behind the counter.

"G'mornin'," the thin man returned without smiling.

"Mind if I take advantage of some of this heat your stove is putting out, suh?"

"He'p yourself."

"Thank ya, suh."

Joshua stood at the rear of the stove, knowing that the front was reserved for white men. The intense heat made his hands tingle with pain, but he didn't move. Even the pain was warming, as he flexed his fingers slowly.

He stared idly around the store. Axes, rifles, hoes, plow tongues, plow lines, bridles, baskets, crosscut saws, two-man saws, wagon tongues, sacks of guano, cotton seed, chicken feed and shovels hung from the rafters, the walls, and rested on the floor. The back of the store was for women: bolts of cloth, thread, needles, sewing machines, hats, bonnets, and things that women didn't talk about around men. The wall behind the counter was filled with shelves of canned goods.

There was a gust of cold air as the door opened, and Joshua looked around the stove to see a white man walk in.

"Cold out there, Ralph!" the newcomer said cheerily.

"Tell me something I don't know, George."

The two men laughed.

George walked over to the stove and stared around it at Joshua, who mumbled a greeting.

The white man didn't respond for a moment, then laughed. "Nigger, you so black, almost can't tell you from the stove."

The white men laughed loudly.

Joshua knew he was supposed to grin and laugh, too, but he could only manage a smile and a soft, "Yas, suh."

"Say," George began, looking intently at Joshua again, "Ain't you Charlie Smith's boy? Live out there off Braxton Pike?"

"Yes, suh."

"I thought that nigger boy looked familiar when he come in," Ralph said from behind the counter. "Been coming in here with his paw since he was a little thing."

"Yes, suh."

"Sorry to hear about your maw," George offered.

"Your maw die?" Ralph asked, surprised.

"Yes, suh. Back in the beginning of the winter."

Ralph nodded. "I believe I did hear something about that." He shook his head. "I've been blessed, George. My maw's still livin'. Be eighty-seven come the third of May."

"My maw be seventy-seven come the twenty-second of October."

Joshua thought about his mother, wondering if she was all right beneath the cold, hard earth. She would've been forty-four in March.

"Heard you'd taken up preaching, boy?" George addressed him from the other side of the stove.

"Yas, suh."

"I overheard one of my niggers say you can preach hellfire and brimstone."

"Thank you, suh," Joshua responded, not displeased.

"I tell you, boy. I like a nigger that can preach. I wish some of them niggers that work for me would get religion or the smallpox or somethin' that would make'em give me a honest day's work."

Joshua said a dull, "Yas, suh," but his mind was wondering how he should ask the man for a job.

"Ain't you kinna young to preach?" Ralph asked from behind the counter.

"Naw, suh," Joshua responded firmly. "Least the Lord don't think so. He the one what called me."

George laughed. "Well, boy, if the Lord called something black as you to preach His word, He knowed what He was doing. I swear, sitting in church on Sunday looking at somethin' black as you would scare hell out of me."

Joshua smiled weakly. He didn't see how he could ask this man for a job. But he had to.

"How you and your brothers getting along?" Ralph asked from behind the counter.

"Not too good, suh," Joshua said, turning to face the counter but making sure he kept his head lowered. "I used up the last of the flour and meal this morning."

Ralph grunted. "Well, why didn't you say so, nigger?"

"Suh?" Joshua asked, bewildered.

"I knowed your paw and he was a good man until he started drinking. And I reckon if God saw fit to call you to preach, then He must see something decent in you. What you need?"

"Whatever you could let us have would be appreciated, suh."

"I know that," Ralph said, irritably. "I asked you, what you need?"

"Flour, meat, meal, vegetables," Joshua said, the words rushing out of him.

Ralph nodded.

"And some warm pants and shirts," Joshua added quickly.

"You had anything to eat this morning?"

"Naw, suh."

"Well, get some cheese and crackers out of that barrel and case next to where Mister George is."

"Thank you, suh."

"You got a wagon?"

"I come to town in it, suh."

Reverend Smith's amazement at the miracle God wrought that morning had not diminished though almost seventy years had passed. Mister Ralph told him to fill his wagon with whatever he needed, and come back when that ran out.

Throughout the winter Joshua went to town twice a month and loaded the wagon. When planting time came, Mister Ralph let him have all the seed and guano he needed. Joshua worked harder than he ever had that spring, summer, and into the fall and, after he sold the cotton, walked into the store and paid Mister Ralph every penny he owed him.

"Reverend Smith?"

Since then he had walked and talked with God daily, trusting in Him with a faith as blind and dense as night.

"Reverend Smith!"

Most folks thought it was enough to just believe in God. You believed in what you could see.

"Reverend SMITH!"

"Huh?" But you couldn't believe in what you couldn't see. You had to have faith and faith was knowing what a sensible man wouldn't believe.

He felt something shaking him and opened his eyes, blinking slowly, hearing his wife call his name. He reached up and took her hand, patting it gently. "How long you been calling me?"

She squeezed his hand softly. "You scared me. I knocked on the door and when you didn't answer, I opened it and saw you sitting in here in the dark. Kept calling your name and you didn't even move. Sitting in here in the dark like this. You scared me!"

He turned and looked out the window. "It's almost dark, isn't it?" he chuckled.

Carlotta chuckled with him. "I just woke up myself. Went in the bedroom to just lie down and rest and next thing I knew, I was waking up. What do you think you want for dinner?"

"Aw, I don't feel like eating anything."

"You have to eat, Reverend Smith."

He patted her hand again. "I'm not hungry," he said softly.

She shook her head. "You worry me."

"Don't worry about me."

"Well, I can't help it. I could boil a chicken breast for you."

"All right. If that'll keep you from worrying."

"It'll help," she said, walking slowly from the room.

Reverend Smith waited a moment before standing up, and as he did, he saw a tiny pinhead of light in the center of a wide expanse of blackness that grew and grew until it threatened to swallow the darkness. He blinked and the bookcase beside the door returned to his vision.

He eased back into the chair, turned on the small desk lamp, and opened the manila folder. He looked at the various drafts of his obituary and placed the one with the 1897 birthdate on top. Then he put the order of his funeral service with the hymns and scripture readings he wanted atop the obituary. On top of all went the papers for his crypt at the mausoleum. He cleared a space in the center of the desk and placed the folder neatly in it.

Death wasn't nothing but a walk into the Light.

Morning

Even with eyes closed and the shades drawn, Reverend Smith could feel the sun poised in the sky like a hawk in the nexus of eternity, ready to plunge to earth hooked, beaked, taloned.

He lay in bed on the morning of that last day in July, eyes closed, listening to the sounds of her from the bathroom. Fifty-six years of listening to the slow trickle of the faucet as she hummed fragments of hymns while washing her face, the weary sigh after she put in her false teeth, the rush of water when she flushed the toilet.

He wanted to pull the adding machine from under her desk in the dining room and figure how many mornings there were in fifty-six years of listening. He would have to subtract the mornings he'd awakened in hotel and motel rooms and, before colored were allowed to stay in hotels and motels, the mornings he awakened in the guest rooms of preachers and church people all over the country. It seemed that there'd been fifty-six years of those mornings, too.

Especially on those mornings he had wished for the sounds of her as familiar as this flaying sun of summer. For better or worse. How many times had he stood before a couple at the altar in a church, in the living room of a house, or on the lawn of a flower-sparkling yard and asked a proud and nervous young man, "Do you take this woman for better or worse, richer or poorer, in sickness and in health, until death do you part?" Always the boy said, "I do," not knowing to what he was agreeing. How could he? The words were wrong. It wasn't a matter of better or worse, but better *and*. After fifty-six years, he didn't know if there was much difference.

He heard the thud of her cane against the carpeted floor and listened as it continued though the bedroom, up the hallway to the dining room and, like the beat of a funeral drum, through the breakfast room and into the kitchen.

She didn't look like a white woman anymore. That skin as milky as magnolia blossoms in the moonlight had yellowed and then browned with age.

They were married on a Sunday afternoon in September in the study of Reverend Collier, the old, graying minister of the colored Baptist church in town, the only preacher he'd ever known who lisped. Reverend Smith had wanted the wedding in his church at the close of service one Sunday morning, but she said no, and didn't give a reason. It was as if she wanted the marriage to be a secret, so that she could have the fact without the change. The only witnesses were Ol' Lady Daniels, her face sealed as tightly as a water barrel, and Reverend Collier's wife, smelling of chicken grease, who cried so much that Reverend Smith began to think he was at a funeral.

It had been a dismal little wedding on an afternoon so cloudy that Reverend Collier had had to light the coal-oil lamps in his study. Reverend Smith was embarrassed even now that it had been his hands which trembled during the ceremony, his lips which stammered and stumbled over the words he was used to telling others to repeat after him. And the ring had slipped from his fingers as he tried to slide it onto her finger and fallen to the floor at her feet where it twinkled up at him like a one-eyed kitten.

She hadn't had a wedding gown, but a simple white dress with a high, frilly neck, her long black hair streaming down her back like a veil. She repeated her vows in a quiet and strong voice frightening in its confidence, especially when she turned, looked at him, and said, "I do." He lowered his eyelids as though he were the bride.

Yet, leaving the minister's study, she slipped her arm through his and, once seated in the carriage he had rented from the livery stable, she kissed him with the warmth of a promise fulfilled.

As the horse clip-clopped slowly along the road, he wanted to apologize for spoiling the ceremony, but Carlotta was not much for words, even back then. Maybe she didn't need them like he did, or didn't trust them, and sensing that she wanted the silence, he allowed it to be.

He lived in a room on the top floor of the colored undertaker's house. He'd insisted on one night alone before they moved out to Ol' Lady Daniels', where Carlotta insisted they live. They wouldn't be there long. He knew that. What kind of man did she think he was to live with his mother-in-law? He had applied for a teaching job in Ford, Arkansas, and even if he didn't get it, he would find some kind of work to supplement the five dollars a week the church paid, anything to support his wife like a man was supposed to.

She followed him up the stairway on the back of the undertaker's house and into his room. It wasn't much. Just a big room with a bed, a dresser, and a writing table with a chair, which the undertaker had gotten for him, because "You a preacher, and I know you need something to sit at and write your sermons, and study your Bible." There was nothing of his in the room, not even photographs of his mother and father, for none existed.

But, after he lit the coal-oil lamp on the little table beside the bed and the one on the desk, she stood in the middle of the room and looked around carefully, slowly, as if it were the most beautiful room she'd ever seen. Then she came to him, not like a scared virgin bride (and she had been a virgin), but with all the certainty of a woman loved, and when he went to blow out the coal-oil lamps, she said, "No. I want to look at you."

So they lay, each staring at the other, her white fingers caressing his dense blackness, his black hands gently kneading her white flesh. There was something almost illicit in the commingling of these two extremes joining as if in defiance of gravity. Against him her whiteness became luminous, and against her, his blackness was as solid and impenetrable as if carved from deepest night.

Then came morning and with it the letter offering him the job as the colored teacher in Ford. They were sitting on the front porch waiting for the colored man from the livery to come and drive them out to Ol' Lady Daniels', when the postman arrived.

After reading the letter he handed it to her, a smile of pride and satisfaction on his lips.

Carlotta read the letter, folded it, and handed it back without comment. The corners of her mouth were as placid as an early spring day.

"I'll have the liv'ry man stop at the Western Union office and I'll send 'em a wire to tell 'em that we'll be there Sunday night," he said, excited. "They said in the letter that they already got us a place to stay."

"What makes you think I'm coming?" she said more than asked.

He stared at her, a wrenching in his gut as if he had swallowed a fiery snake.

She stared out at the road, an aura of remoteness surrounding her like a bridal veil.

"You knew I had applied for the job," he protested, his voice suddenly high-pitched and almost whining. "You never said a word about not coming."

"Never said I would, either."

"So what was I supposed to think?"

"Think what you want. Whatever made you think I would leave Momma?"

Maybe that was when the love began, not with a deluge of emotion as sweet as strawberry Kool-Aid but in an agonizing hopelessness and a despair without end.

It had not been an easy marriage, or even a happy one. But he had married her, and marrying her for her white skin was as good a reason as any, because all the reasons were false. Back then, you married and you spent your life learning what a marriage was. You learned where the soft, velvety parts were in the other person, and where the hard, cold places were, too, and you learned how to stroke the one, and how not to run your head into the other too often. And if you weren't happy some of the time, or most of the time, there was, through the years, a knowing and a being known, and if that didn't add up to happiness, it was a comfort and maybe that was better.

He supposed she had married him for his skin, too, though what mystery and wonder could there have been in his blackness? "That nigger is so black he makes coal look like vanilla ice cream," she'd told him her mother had said.

That had hurt him, but later, after he came to love Ol' Lady Daniels and Carlotta, he understood. Understanding didn't always stop the hurting, but it helped him accept that Ol' Lady Daniels and Carlotta sat apart from the world, observed, and announced their conclusions with all the calmness of truth that could not be challenged.

That was why everybody spoke of her as Ol' Lady Daniels. She couldn't have been fifty even when Reverend Smith met her, but she had already abrogated to herself the prerogative of old age and said what she thought, regardless of who you thought you were.

Being a widow woman had had something to do with it. Carlotta had never known her father, had not a memory of him even, and Ol' Lady Daniels painted no pictures her daughter could have mistaken for memory.

She reminded him of Tremble. She owned a hundred acres of prime farmland and orchards, on which many of the colored worked. Everybody said she was a good boss lady who paid a fair wage for a good day's work and didn't have anybody working on shares. How had she managed to raise four children, keep a hundred acres of prime land producing, and at the same time, keep the Ku Kluxers from running her off in the middle of the night at a time when they chased colored out of the South if they didn't like the way you walked? Why hadn't she sold the land, moved North, and passed for white? He never asked, because no one asked her questions. She would tell the truth.

Whites were scared of her, too. In stores white men called her "ma'am" and "Mrs. Daniels," though they knew she was colored, and in those days whites never called colored women anything but "Auntie" or by their first names.

How many times had he sat on the porch with her and Carlotta and seen someone come to the gate, a good two, three hundred yards from the porch, and carry on a shouted conversation with her, not daring to come in the yard unless she invited them? White nor colored walked through that gate without her invitation, and he never saw her give it.

He had gotten up the courage once to ask, "Sister Daniels? Why didn't you invite Brother Edmonds on the porch instead of shouting back and forth like that? It would've been easier on your vocal cords, wouldn't it?" he hastened to add, chuckling nervously.

"Maybe," she allowed, "but what I want that nigger in my yard for?"

It was said without contempt or condescension, or even emotion. To her it was a self-evident truth.

He stared at the ceiling where brown watermarks spread across the wallpaper like a nest of dragons. From the kitchen he heard the sound of applause and laughter and wondered which game show she had on. She never watched the TV, but kept it on all day for the sound.

He pulled back a corner of the sheet and slid his legs over the edge of the bed. Just five years ago he would've been up by now, had breakfast, and been outside, mowing the lawn, pruning his tomato plants, weeding the flowers, picking bugs off the turnip, mustard, and collard greens. But he'd stopped mowing the lawn after the heart attack three years ago. He had managed to get a few tomato plants and pole beans in before his stroke last summer, only to watch them shrivel like worms in alcohol.

Bending over, it was a moment before his fingers could grasp the wooden cane beside the bed. He raised himself slowly and stood until he could balance securely on what felt like cat whiskers. Cautiously he put the cane forward, dragging his right leg after, and made his way to the bathroom.

After washing his face, he took the electric razor from the shelf above the sink. He pushed at the switch with his thumb, but couldn't move it. He bit at his lower lip and clutched harder at the square razor, pushing as hard as he could at the switch. His hand trembled as if rebelling against being asked to do what was beyond its capacity. He grabbed the wrist with his left hand and both hands quivered like a bird in winter snow.

"Why don't you let me shave you, Reverend Smith?"

He gasped. "You scared me," he said angrily, turning to see Carlotta standing in the doorway, leaning on her metal cane. "How long have you been standing there looking at me?" he wanted to know, letting his arms drop to his sides.

She looked at the anger in his eyes. "I haven't been

standing here staring at you," she said. "I wouldn't do that," she added softly. "I came back just to see if you were awake yet."

His anger receded like the flame on a nub of candle flickering as it went out.

"Why don't you come sit on the bed and let me shave you?"

Shame and gratitude suffused his features, and embarrassed, he tried to smile. "Aw, that's all right. Shaving is one of those things that doesn't feel right unless I do it myself."

She nodded.

"And it seems like I should be able to do *something* for myself," he admitted, looking at her with a frightening helplessness.

"It takes time," she said sympathetically. "Last year this time you couldn't even raise your right arm. You've come a long way. You were as close to death as I've seen you."

And he wondered if she still saw death clinging to him like a greasy film on dishes already washed.

Through her eyes he could see how loosely the pajamas hung on his body, the fly open, exposing the white knots of kinky pubic hair like dull globs of spit against the black of his crotch. He pulled his pajama bottoms up and the electric razor fell from his hand to the floor. He stared at her with an unworded plea.

"If you'd known I'd end up like this, you probably wouldn't have married me," he said and tried to laugh.

"I ought to say no, just so you won't say something ridiculous like that again," she said softly. "Don't you know after all these years?"

"I don't know what I know anymore."

"You'll feel better after you have some breakfast."

"I'm not hungry."

"You have to eat, Reverend Smith," she insisted.

He nodded, but only to prevent the lecture that would come if he didn't relent.

"Your bacon and eggs will be ready in a little while. How about some grapefruit juice this morning?"

"Whatever you say," he answered dully.

He watched as she made her way slowly up the hallway. At least she hadn't humiliated him by offering to pick up the razor. That didn't solve the problem of how he was going to get it off the floor. Perhaps if he held on to the side of the sink, he could lower himself enough to try and grasp it. But he didn't know if he could pull himself back up, or even if there was the strength in his arm to hold on to the sink while reaching for the razor. Last week a big horsefly had gotten in the kitchen and he had swatted at it with a rolled-up newspaper, missed, and fallen to the floor. Carlotta had finally had to go next door and get Ralph to come and help him up.

He pushed at the razor with his foot and slid it a few inches across the carpet. Grasping the cane from where it hung over the edge of the basin, he went into the bedroom, pushing the razor before him. With a final push, he shoved it under the bed and slumped wearily on the edge of the mattress.

"Reverend Smith! Where're you going?"

"Out!" he called, not turning to look at her.

"The paper is right here on the breakfast-room table if that's what you want."

"I know that," he said testily.

"Well, I don't see what you want to go outside for. It's ninety-two already and they said it was going to reach a hundred today."

"I'll be all right," he said wearily as the heat through the screen door seared him like a blowtorch.

He stepped carefully onto the porch, closing the door

behind him. He had dressed as he had on any other day of his eighty years—a white suit, white shirt, black tie, and straw hat. Anyone driving past would've thought he was going somewhere, and maybe he needed them to think that.

Leaning heavily on the cane, he made his way off the porch just as Ralph came out of his house.

"How you this morning, Reverend?" Ralph called loudly, hurrying across the driveway separating their houses.

"Well, Ralph. What you saying about yourself?" Reverend Smith smiled.

"Can't complain. How're you getting along?"

"Percolating like weak coffee, but I'm still here."

The two men laughed.

Ralph Johnson had been the second colored on the block. A stocky man with a round face and a thin mustache that made his warm smile appear even wider, he'd just gotten married when he moved next door with his new bride and mother. Reverend Smith had buried the mother, christened the children, married them, and christened the two grandbabies.

"I hope you not coming out here this morning to think about mowing your lawn or clip your hedges. This heat would make a camel look for shade. I'll come over tomorrow and do the lawn and hedges for you."

Reverend Smith smiled and nodded. "All right. I just thought I'd come outside for a few minutes. You know it's hard for me to stay in the house as much as I traveled in my life."

"That's the truth!" Ralph exclaimed sympathetically. "Well, you can rest on your laurels now."

"How's the family?" Reverend Smith asked, ignoring the well-intentioned advice he heard too often.

"Everybody's fine. How's Miz Smith today?"

"Fine, fine."

"Good. Well, Reverend, you have a good day and I'll get to your lawn tomorrow."

"All right, Ralph. You have a good day, too."

"Yes, sir."

He watched Ralph hurry across his yard and get into his car. He beeped his horn and waved as he backed out of the driveway and accelerated down the street.

Ralph had never asked a dime for the work he did for Reverend Smith, not even gas money for taking Carlotta shopping every week, or him to the drugstore for cigars. He offered to pay him, but knew why Ralph didn't accept.

They never talked about it. Reverend Smith found it hard enough now to believe that Ralph had had cancer and been given six months to live. That was eight years ago and Ralph still thought he owed Reverend Smith something. He didn't. Carlotta wouldn't have known what he'd done if Ralph's wife hadn't told her and when she asked him about it, he just said it wasn't anything to talk about.

It wasn't.

The first time was before he met her, when he was just a young preacher in Ouichitta, not even a real preacher but a sixteen-year-old boy who had been touched by the fire and preached the three Sundays every month when the preacher didn't come.

That first time was as hot as today. The old ladies sat on the first pew like they always did, in their starched white dresses, fanning with little white handkerchiefs. He wouldn't preach long, not because it was hot but because Sister Adams had told him after he'd preached a long sermon one Sunday, "Son, you preach pretty good for a young fella, but you don't know enough yet to preach as long as you preached this morning." She was right and after that he kept his sermons to fifteen or twenty minutes, long enough to get the church chorusing Amens and Hallelujahs and Thank You, Jesuses.

That morning he preached the text, "I am the way, the truth and the life," and talked about the way being like the road that ran by the church and that if you wanted to get to town you had to stay on the way, because if you went off into the woods you might get bit by a snake or get lost, and he preached about the truth as something you knew inside you. You didn't need any county agent telling you when to put your cottonseed in the ground because it was something you knew. He reminded them of the year the old white agent had come and asked them why they hadn't put their cottonseed in yet, 'cause it was time, but something told them not to but that something didn't tell them why and he called them a bunch of hard-headed niggers. The white bossman come out the next day and told'em he was going to kick'em all off the land if they didn't get to planting and they said yassuh and didn't drop one seed in the ground. That weekend a rain come up like no one had ever seen and some of'em started wondering if they should get to building arks. Ol' man Jerry Douglas swore up and down that he'd caught a wide-mouthed bass in all the water standing in his cabbage patch. Three days later when the sun finally came out, the white bossman was there and he was just so happy, bragging about how smart his niggers were because the niggers on the other plantations had put their seed in the ground and it had all washed away or rotted. That's what truth was. You knew something that you couldn't explain and nobody could argue out of you and that was the kind of truth Jesus was and then he started preaching about life. He had planned to talk about how, if the heart was what gave your body life, Jesus was the heart in your soul, but he had scarcely started on that part when something like a cold electric current went through his body and he started pacing back and forth across the pulpit shouting, "Jesus is the Life!" "Jesus is the Life!" and he jumped off the pulpit and paced up and down the aisles until the whole congregation was chanting "Jesus is the Life! Jesus is the Life!" shouting and crying "Thank you, Jesus! Thank you, Jesus!" He took Sister Sarah Adams by her gnarled hands, Sister Adams who had taught his daddy in school and taught him and he lifted her from the pew and she stood beside him, her old body bent and twisted like a forgotten life. "Jesus!" he shouted over the screaming exultant tumult, "Jesus! Come down here this morning and take this body that's all bent over with the artheritis and the rheumatics and make it straight! JESUS, put your healing spirit on Sister Adams, JESUS!" and suddenly, her body twitched like the tail of a snake and she shivered like a cold wind had come through the windows and the cane fell from her hands and her body straightened and she took one step, and another, and yet another until she was strutting up and down the aisles like a bantam rooster with new hens. "Thank you, Jesus!" she shouted, tears coming down her face. "Thank you! Thank you!"

After church the people didn't go out front and chat like usual but rushed up to touch his sleeve, kiss his hands, or just gaze on his face.

"The spirit of the Lawd is sho' 'nuf in you, Joshua!"

"Son, you shone with a mighty light this mawning."

He nodded automatically as they pressed around him, a grin on his face because that seemed like the appropriate response, but all he wanted was to go home and sleep off the fatigue that was like great and heavy weights dragging at his limbs. He wondered if he was coming down with a summer cold, because he was chilly and the faces surrounding him were blurred and indistinct, and he couldn't wholly remember all that had happened.

He knew that Sister Adams had been healed, it seemed,

but he hadn't planned to do that, or even tried to do it. It had just happened. If it had.

He remembered Poppa taking him once to a revival-tent meeting in town, where a colored evangelist was healing people. Coming back home that night in the wagon, he was sleepy but had to stay awake, because Poppa was angry about "that no-'count nigger coming here claiming he can heal. He getting folks all excited and anybody with a brain in they heads could see that that tumor he said he taken out of that big fat woman wasn't nothing but a hog bladder he had wrapped up in something in his pocket. That nigger ought to be ashamed of hisself coming in here and taking advantage of ignorant sharecroppers."

Joshua knew that he hadn't tricked anybody, because Sister Adams was still walking around and around the church like she was leading the Fourth of July parade in town. Now different ones were asking him to come pray over their mother who was low sick in bed, and one woman asked him to straighten her husband's arm what had gotten broke when he was a boy and growed back together crooked, and Joshua started to tremble from the chill in his body.

He felt an arm encircle his shoulder, an arm as hard as stone, and a voice like a stone in his ear. "Y'all go on and leave this boy be." He recognized Brother Emory's voice. "We done seed a miracle here this morning, and that ought to be enough for one Sunday. God used this here boy to ease some of Sister Sarah's misery, and look to me like the boy done been about used up for today."

"You right about that, Brother Emory."

"I bring my husband over to see you tomorrow, Joshua," a woman with a big straw hat with a big feather in it said.

"Mary Lou, you just go on," Brother Emory said lazily. "I been knowing Bud since his momma was big with him and it was not wanting to work made his arm draw him up like that."

"Brother Emory, you ought to be 'shamed," somebody said out of the general laughter.

"He sho' outa," Mary Lou responded, not amused.

"Y'all go on with yourselves," Brother Emory prodded gently. "Everything is in God's hands."

So the people drifted away, and as they did, Joshua heard himself sigh with relief.

"How you feel, son?" Brother Emory asked, taking his arm from Joshua's shoulders.

"Tired. Sleepy. I was feeling chilly, but I feels better now."

Brother Emory nodded. "You bring your wagon this morning?"

"No, sir. It was pretty out, so I walked."

"Well, I got my wagon out back. You don't look to me like you should walk back. Come on."

Joshua followed him gladly through the side door and to the grove of shade trees behind the church where Brother Emory's mule and wagon stood.

It was a hot, still Sunday afternoon. The sun seemed stuck in the sky from where it would pour down heat forever. Brother Emory had on his bib overalls without a shirt and he slapped at a horsefly that had dared alight on his bare arm. He flicked the dead fly onto the dusty ground with a grunt of satisfaction and settled himself on the wagon seat.

"Reach behind that seat there, son, and hand me my hat. I don't want this sun to boil away what little sense I got left."

Joshua looked behind the seat and saw a beat-up straw cowboy hat and handed it to the old man with muscles hard as sorrow. Brother Emory slapped the mule's rump gently with the lines and with a jerk, the wagon rolled slowly out of the grove and into the sun.

The wagon creaked along the road and the further it got

69

from the church and the small crowd of people standing in front and staring after it, the warmer Joshua felt. Soon, a fine sheen of perspiration glazed his forehead and a trickle of sweat ran from his armpit down his side. He felt like himself again.

Brother Emory sat stooped on the wagon seat, his head almost down between his shoulders, the lines held loosely in his hands, and Joshua wondered if he'd fallen asleep or even died until he heard him humming softly, humming a strange melody Joshua didn't recognize.

"That's one of the way-back songs," Brother Emory said suddenly, as if knowing that Joshua had been listening. "I ain't thought of that one in fifty, sixty years. Never did like it much, to tell the truth. And it still gives me the chills." He shook himself as if to ward off some menacing cold rising unbidden from within him. "It's strange I should even remember it, son, 'cause I remembers hearing it only once or twice."

The mule had settled into a pace which was only fast enough to keep the wagon wheels turning, as if it knew that Brother Emory had something serious to say and it wanted to hear, too.

"I was born deep back in slavery time," Brother Emory continued, sitting up straighter on the seat. "Some of these folks around here make like they know what slavery was about, but most of 'em was still eating at the trough when Massa Lincoln freed us slaves. You probably don't know nothing 'bout no trough, but back in them times, food for the slave chillun, all what was too young to work, was put in a pig trough and the chillun got down on their hands and knees just like they was little pigs and ate their meals that way. When I thinks back on it, it makes me kind of mad, but in them days, I reckon us thought nothing of it. That was just how things was.

"Me and Brother Simpson 'bout the only ones in these parts what go deep back into slavery. He was a gravedigger in slavery times, too. I tease him sometimes about how much he like dead folk. He say somebody got to see to their comfort." He hummed the melody again, took a red bandanna from his back pocket, and wiped his forehead.

"I don't know whether Simpson would remember what I'm going to tell you or not," he continued, stuffing the bandanna back in his pocket. "He was there, but I can't remember if he was there the night it all started. But he might not remember. We has different ways of taking care of the dead.

"Now, back in them times, colored didn't have no churches. Three or four times a year ol' massa would take all us slaves to church. White folks wouldn't come that Sunday and the white preacher would preach us a special sermon about how us was supposed to obey the massa and the missus and if we did, we could serve massa and missus up in heaven. Well, they must've thought us was fools to believe something like that." He chuckled, and the mule's ears twitched. "I remember this time—it was the Fourth of July. That was always a time Massa Wellington brung us to church, 'cepting there was so many of us slaves that the church couldn't hold us all. So church would be held in the big field right next to it, the same one that's there now. Then, after church was over, some of the slaveowners would make a speech about how it was the Fourth of July and that meant us niggers was freed from being savages in Africa and would be civilized like white folks one day as long as we obeyed the massa and the missus. After all the speeching was done, there'd be plenty of bar-b-que, whiskey, and what-all. Somebody would've brought a fiddle or two and we'd dance and have a good time.

"Well, Boxer put an end to all that. Reverend McGinnis

was the white preacher. He was a tall, lean white man, face like a dried cornstalk, and he was about as big around as one. This Fourth of July he was preaching all that to us about obeying the massa and missus and how lucky we would be to die and go to Heaven and wait on them there and he was just going on and on and suddenly Boxer stood up.

"We thought he was getting up to go on off in the bushes and do his business. But he didn't move. Just stood there, sun shining on his black, bald head like the light coming off a train engine at midnight.

"Must've been a thousand slaves there from all the different plantations that was around here then, and we was all sitting on the grass, and some of the young ones were up in the trees. I'd seen a few of the young ones slip off in the woods, though, and I thought that Boxer had stood up to see where one of his granddaughters was. One of 'em, Pearline, was one pretty black girl. When old men died with smiles on their lips we figured they'd died thinking about Pearline. But I looked around and seen Pearline sitting on the grass near the church building with a yellow rag tied around her head. So Boxer wasn't looking for her.

"Boxer was an old man, though he didn't look it. Folks think I'm old, but Boxer was old as Noah, and my daddy told me that Boxer was already old when Andy Jackson went down to New Orleans. That was befo' my time, but my daddy could remember up on ol' Andy. You can look up in one of your schoolbooks and find out when that was.

"Everybody called him Boxer, 'cause that was what he done. Massa Wellington and the other slaveowners would have fights between they biggest and strongest slaves and bet money on which one would win. Boxer was so good with his fists that massa didn't allow him to work in the fields or do nothing else 'cept eat good food, and exercise so he could fight. I reckon ol' massa made more money off Boxer than he did from cotton. Massa would take him to Jackson, New Orleans, Mobile, even far away as Atlanta. Heard he even took him to Charleston once. Wasn't no slave nowhere ever whupped him, either.

"Even if he was old as God, he still looked like he could whup anybody in the world standing there in the hot sun with no shirt on so everybody could see his muscles. Boxer had muscles that would've made a racehorse jealous. And he was big as night and blacker and he just stood there, staring at Reverend McGinnis with eyes that seemed like they was buzzing like a hornet's nest.

"Reverend McGinnis' voice got weaker and weaker until he just stopped and I could see the little beads of sweat popping out on his brow. I looked up at Massa Wellington who was sitting up on the stage with the other slaveowners and he was sweating a little, too, 'cause he must've thought that Boxer had taken a mind to wring his neck.

"It got real quiet and everybody just waited to see what Boxer was up to. Finally, he laughed, but wasn't no fun in Boxer's laugh. His voice was deep and low and when that laugh came rolling out, it sounded like thunder and some of us looked up even though there wasn't a cloud in the sky.

" 'We ain't waiting on white folks in heaven,' Boxer said suddenly, his voice cracking like a whip on a slave's back. 'You hear me, Reverend McGinnis? Ain't waiting on white folks in heaven. Ain't beating up on niggers for'em, either, massa. And if any white folks up there try and make us niggers wait on'em, I'll throw they asses straight to hell!' And he sat back down."

Brother Emory laughed loudly, taking his red bandanna from his back pocket and wiping his eyes. "Son, we thought that white preacher was going to die right there on the little

73

makeshift stage his slaves had built. He didn't know what to say. His mouth was moving like a fish's out of water and like a fish, no words come out, and us slaves was sitting there just waiting to see what was going to happen next, half scared and half happy, too, and then, somebody—it was probably one of the young folk—started laughing, and that did it. All us slaves just bust out laughing, and son, you get a thousand colored people laughing, you got you some laughing. Massa Wellington got so red looked like all the blood was going to ooze out of his face.

"That was the end of church that day. He stomped off the platform and Reverend McGinnis tried to stomp off, and that was the last Fourth of July sermon we ever got. Well, wasn't no more than a month later, either, that Boxer died. He was sitting on his porch one evening and kinna sighed, and that was it. We had his funeral the next night and afterward, we was sitting around in the slave quarters and somebody pointed up in the sky at a shooting star and said, 'Look like Boxer just throwed a white man into hell,' and we must've laughed the rest of that night. And to this day, I can't see a shooting star without thinking, Boxer done throwed another one.''

Joshua laughed, unknotted his tie, and loosened the top button of his shirt.

"Well, we didn't need the white folks' church and didn't want it. Had our own church. Didn't have no church building and didn't need one. Once you put religion in a building, folks get so busy attending to the building they forgits they religion. I know when I die the folks around here will finally put a coat of paint on our church building, and after that, somebody will put a piano in it, and after that they be talking about stained-glass windows! But they got enough sense to wait until I'm dead, 'cause they know I'm old enough and crazy enough to come up there one night and tear the building down. I told'em once that the reason they wanted a pretty church was so they could keep God in it and not let Him into their houses. Brother Emory chuckled. "They didn't like that too much. Your daddy did, though. That was when he was our preacher. He told'em, 'God ain't about being pretty. God is about truth and truth is ugly. Ain't nobody slapping no whitewash on the church while I'se still preacher here.' "

Brother Emory chuckled warmly at the memory and reached in the top pocket of his coveralls and pulled out a round box of snuff. He twisted the top off, and knocked a small amount inside his lower lip.

"Back in slavery time," he continued, putting the box of snuff back in his pocket, "our church was out in the woods. There's parts of the Wellington plantation to this day so growed up that white folks is scared to go in'em, and back in slavery time there was even more. Didn't matter to us. We figured couldn't nothing worse happen to us at night than what happened during the day.

"There is a big stand of pine trees way on the other side of where the Jackson Pike is now. Them trees been there since Adam. Biggest trees I ever seed, and at night they looked so tall that I reckon the moon had to pull up her skirts to get over the tops.

"Well, that was our place. Was a clearing in the middle of that stand of pine and we'd build us a fire and sing and pray and testify 'til our souls was satisfied. Sometimes our souls wouldn't be satisfied 'til the sun was coming up and we'd go on to the field and work all day and the ol' overseer would want to know how come we was smiling and so happy that day. Done spent some time with the Lawd, that's how come.

"Now, I don't know what year it was, 'cause what did us care about years. Wasn't nothing gon' be different any year, so we didn't keep track. I know I was grown and had jumped the broom with Bernice. And it was before she got sold away. That's as close as I can date it for you.

"This particular night we just had to go to the woods. Sometimes we went 'cause it made us feel good to sing and pray. Other times we *had* to go or else we wasn't sure we was gon' make it through the next day. This night was like that." He leaned over the side and spat tobacco juice.

"There was a boy on the plantation named Dumb Tom. Everybody called him that, 'cause he wasn't right in the head. Didn't nobody mean him no harm by the name. Everybody looked out for him, 'cause he didn't all the time understand something the overseer or massa might want him to do, and we'd do it for him, help him with it, you know, and cover for him any way we could.

"Well, this particular day ol' overseer—Brad Darnell was his name. Nothing but po' white trash. Wore an ol' straw hat with a hole in the front of the brim, and always had a chaw of tobacco in his cheek. He must've had a falling out with his missus that morning or something, 'cause he knowed how it was with Dumb Tom and knowed we took care of him. And Darnell never cared long as Tom's task of work got done.

"On this day Darnell had sent about ten of us down to start clearing some new ground and told us to take Tom. Now he knowed and we knowed that clearing new ground is hard and dirty work and Tom couldn't do that kind of work. He could scrap cotton, but not clear no new ground. So when we got down there, we told him to find hisself a tree to rest against and take it easy.

"To this day I don't know how come we didn't hear Darnell coming, but we didn't. First thing we knowed there he was and he seen Tom setting under a tree sound asleep, and he unwound his ol' bullwhip and started lashing the boy. Lawd, have mercy! He whupped that boy until the blood dripping on the leaves around the tree sounded like raindrops. And when he finished, he told us we bet not move him until nightfall or he'd give us some of the same.

"Soon as he was out of sight, we put down our axes and saws and rope and what-all and decided that if Darnell wanted to whip us, we would just have to take it, 'cause if we let that boy lie there 'til night, he would be dead, if he wasn't already. After making sure that Darnell wasn't sneaking around spying on us, four of us carried Tom back to the quarters to Madame Couseau, who was the healer."

They had reached the side road which led to Joshua's house, but Brother Emory didn't even glance at it. "Why don't you take supper at my house today? I bring you back toward evening."

Joshua nodded eagerly.

"I was one of the four what carried Tom and my hands and wrists was slick with blood. Well, we left him with Madame Couseau, like I said, and went on back down to clear new ground, not that much work was going to get done the rest of that day.

"Late that afternoon Darnell come back and seen that Tom was gone. But he didn't say nothing. Took one look at us and went on away. I think he could tell that we wasn't in no mood to be messed with by then and if he'd tried anything, I swear I believe one of us would've killed him. I ain't saying I would've been the one, but I can't say I wouldn't have either.

"Come night, didn't nobody feel like eating, even though we was hungry, but everybody in the quarter knew what had happened and word from Madame Couseau was that he probably wouldn't live through the night. Didn't nobody have to say nothing about having a prayer meeting that night. Everybody just knowed. Our souls was so heavy, we was walking around like the whip had ripped our flesh.

"There must've been fifty, maybe a hundred of us who

made our way back to our church in the woods that night and there was some sho'-'nuf singing and praying, some hard praying asking the Lawd to come down and put a plague on the white folks like he done the Egyptians.

"I don't recollect how long we'd been singing and praying. I wasn't keeping track of the North Star that night. But it had been a while when we heard a noise and our first thought was that Darnell had sent patterollers to get us. We looked around at each other and I saw different ones feeling around on the ground for a stick, a rock, or anything. If it was them, we was ready for a fight.

"It got real quiet and we was all looking at where the noise was coming from and who should step into the clearing but Dumb Tom's momma, Ora. And behind her was Madame Couseau, and then come her daughter, Delilah, and behind her come four men carrying Tom."

Brother Emory stopped and took out his bandanna again to wipe his forehead, but Joshua wasn't sure that he wasn't wiping at his eyes, too.

"Po' Ora. You know, son, I thinks about a lot of things, and one of the things I like to figure out is how come each person was born. Way I figure it, God put everybody here for a purpose and if they can figure out what that purpose is all about, they can walk the right road. And I'm pretty good at figuring that out, too. Some folks purpose is to dig graves, like Simpson. That man can dig a pretty grave, and when he put the dirt back in, he makes sure the mound on top is all rounded off nice and neat. Now, you take Mary Lou's husband, Bud, the one with the crooked arm she want you to straighten. His purpose is telling jokes. I ain't never heard nobody tell a funny story as good as Bud. But he don't know that and probably never will, 'cause something happen to his arm once and he been feeling sorry for hisself ever since.

"But Ora. Ora's the only one I ever knowed that I couldn't figure out her purpose, unless a body's purpose could be to have misery. When Ora died, I think all us slaves was happy for her. But by then, it didn't matter 'cause she was plumb crazy. And it was Tom's whupping that drove her crazy. You could see it in her eyes that night, 'cause they just kept rolling around and round in her head like spinning marbles. She hadn't been much older than Tom, you see, when the overseer, the one before Darnell, took the whip to her. He made all us slaves come and watch that one.

"You too young to know about womens yet, but Ora was a pretty little brownskin gal. Just as ripe and sweet-looking as fresh watermelon. Reason I know is 'cause the overseer ripped her dress off and tied her hands to a stake and we all saw how ripe and sweet she looked, if you get my meaning. Overseer took his whip and he was proud of what a expert he was with a whip. We used to see him practicing sometimes, putting tin cans and jars on a fence rail and flicking them off with the tip of the whip.

"He was an expert sho' 'nuf. He didn't use nothing but the tip of that whip and he turned one of her breasts into a bloody pulp. POP! And she would scream! POP! And she would scream and when he finished, one breast was hanging down like it was a pig being bled. And the other breast was just as firm and nice, the nipple sticking out like it was looking for a suckling baby.

"None of us never knowed for sure just what Ora had done to bring on a whipping like that, but we suspicioned that the ol' overseer had come to her in the night and she wouldn't have him. After the whipping, Ora wasn't any good for a year until she got Tom. His momma was sold away and Ora just took him and raised him like he was hers. She got better, but it seemed like the whipping Tom got just brought everything back and she snapped."

The wagon came to a sudden stop and Brother Emory looked up with a start. He chuckled. "Ol' Myra know where home is even if I don't." They stood in the yard of a small cabin.

"The houses back on the plantation looked like this. Folks used to ask me how come I didn't build myself something bigger, or leastways different." He laughed. "To tell the truth, I didn't think about it. I went to the lumberyard with all the money I had and gave it to the man and told him to give me what he could for the money. And every board he give me is in this house. Wasn't 'til I finished it that I realized, 'Lawd, I done built myself back into slavery, now ain't I?' But that's all right. Lot of these folks 'shamed of where they come from. What I got to be 'shamed of? I didn't born myself into slavery. Come on in, son."

Joshua found himself in a medium-sized room with a large fireplace against one wall. The walls were covered with a rose-patterned paper and the sunlight through the two front windows made the room bright. Along the wall opposite the fireplace was a single bed, and against the back wall were two tables, one on each side of the back door. On one sat a pan and a bucket of water. Next to the other were two chairs.

Brother Emory took one of the chairs and offered it to Joshua.

"I can't offer you a whole table full of fried chicken or nothing like that. Man my age don't have much use for a whole lot of food. But I got some greens here and can make you some ashcakes like I used to do back in slavery."

Joshua shook his head. "I'm not really hungry, to tell the truth."

"Now, a boy your age got to eat. Don't be telling me you not hungry just 'cause you sitting there thinking you don't want to put an ol' man to no trouble."

Joshua smiled. "It's not that. I'm really not hungry."

Brother Emory looked at him suspiciously for a minute.

"And I can't think about nothing 'til I hear the rest of the story."

Brother Emory chuckled, pleased. "Well, let's take these chairs out back under that ellum tree and sit in the shade."

When they were seated, Brother Emory continued.

"Like I was saying, we was around the fire when Ora, Madame Couseau, Delilah, and the men come in carrying Tom. Madame Couseau had washed off his wounds and put one of her salves on'em, but they was still as red raw as fresh butchered meat. The mens laid Tom next to the fire and Ora fell down beside him and started crying something awful. She had on a loose dress and when she bent over, all us could see down her bosom and see her one good breast and the one that looked like a strip of dried beef hanging from a rafter in a barn. She looked over at Madame Couseau, tears coming out of her eyes, the snot hanging from her nose, and said, 'You can save my boy, Madame. I know you can. You got the power to make him get up and walk. Please help my boy! Please!'

"Madame Couseau was a little bitty black woman. Massa had bought her in New Orleans long time befo' I was born. She wore a white cloth wrapped around her head all the time. Her eyes were sunk back in her skull like she was already dead and she had a voice that sounded like bones rubbing against each other. All us was scared of her, 'cause even though she knowed all about herbs and potions and took care of all our ailments, folks said she knowed other kinds of things, too, and she had been hexing the white folks in New Orleans and that was why Massa Wellington was able to buy her cheap.

"Now, I remember slavery, but Madame Couseau remembered Africa and that's the other reason us was scared

81

of her. When you went to her for a salve or something, she'd mix it up, talking to herself in what we figured must be African. Sometimes, late up in the night, she would start singing in African, and if you woke up and heard it, you had trouble getting back to sleep. You couldn't understand the words, but understanding ain't always in the words, son, and we just knowed she was singing about her home and that would get all us to wondering if we was ever gon' have a home that was ours sho' 'nuf and next morning there'd be a whole lot of folks going to the fields with sad faces.

"Delilah was her daughter and she was born right there on the plantation, but no one ever knowed who the father was. Some said wasn't no father. Said Madame Couseau had gotten the spirits to give her the girl. I don't truck with that kind of nonsense, but then again, there was something different about Delilah.

"She didn't remember Africa for herself, but she knowed it. It was in her face, 'cause when she was just about the age to start having her monthlies, her momma put all kinds of cuts in her face. Said in Africa that was what they did to a girl when she became a woman, said it made her beautiful. Didn't look beautiful to us, scarring that girl's face all up.

"Delilah was tall and black like she come straight from Africa. Tall and thin as a whistling sound on a dark road at midnight. She had big round eyes that seemed like they didn't see nothing and saw everything, too. Her momma had taught her all about the healing herbs and Delilah was about as good as her, too.

"Well, when Ora asked Madame Couseau to do more than put some salves on Tom, we got kinna scared. We'd heard that Madame Couseau had truck with all kinds of African gods that could take all us slaves back to Africa if

82

they'd wanted to, and how come they didn't beats me. But Madame Couseau just looked at Ora and shook her head.

"That made Ora carry on all the more, but Madame Couseau's eyes were like burnt-up stars. Then Delilah said something to her momma in African and that was the first any of us ever knowed that Delilah could talk it. We didn't know what they were saying, but any fool could see that they was arguing, and it seemed to me that they was carrying on an argument they'd done had earlier, befo' they brung Tom out to where we was.

"Delilah said something to her momma that sounded sho'-'nuf angry and then she wheeled around and started toward the fire, and Madame Couseau yelled out, 'Don't you do it, girl! Don't you do it!'

"Delilah didn't pay her no mind and moved over beside the fire where Ora was kneeling over Tom, and she touched Ora on the shoulder and motioned her away. Then, Delilah stood real erect and it seemed to us that she started getting taller and taller until her head was keeping company with the tops of the pine trees and she started chanting and praying in African in a voice thin as a pine needle and it seemed like she got just as thin 'til she just blended with the night and there wasn't nothing but her voice and it seemed to be coming from the center of the fire and going straight up to heaven and some of the other slaves caught the spirit, though they couldn't catch the words, and they started moaning and humming and clapping they hands and swaying back and forth and the next thing we knowed, Dumb Tom was getting up off the ground and there wasn't no cuts on his body and it was like there never had been.

"Somebody screamed—and, son, to tell the truth, it might've been me—and a couple of folks fainted and others were shouting Hallelujah and praising Jesus, but wasn't no Jesus in what Delilah done. But I seen Delilah look over at her momma with a little smile on her lips. But Madame Couseau didn't smile back. She just turned around and marched on away from there.

"Folks started singing and clapping they hands, and Tom was grinning and laughing and po' Ora. Seemed like Tom rising up like that hurt her mind more than helped it, 'cause she started screaming and beating on Tom with her fists and folks had to pull her away and somebody slapped her hard a couple of times and carried her on back to the quarters.

"A few of us started drifting away after that, feeling worse than when we come. Then, somebody, and I wish I could remember who, started singing:

> *'I believe that the Lawd has laid His hands on you,*
> *Hands on you, hands on you.*
> *I believe that the Lawd has laid His hands on you,*
> *And that can be a terrible thing.'"*

It was the song Joshua had heard him humming in the wagon, and hearing it with its words, Joshua shuddered involuntarily. Brother Emory's singing voice was weathered not only with age but with age's memory and as he sang the slow, mournful song, Joshua found himself licking his lips, which were suddenly dry, and trying to swallow, and was afraid when he found he couldn't.

"After that night," Brother Emory continued, "Delilah went around healing folks like she was baking biscuits for a party at the Big House. Every night she was going out to the woods and healing folks. Some of us started staying away, 'cause we didn't feel right about it. Or maybe we didn't feel right about her.

"Sharie died close to Christmastime. She was a mulatto girl. One of massa's boy's slave chillun and just as pretty as she could be. Black curly hair, big gray eyes. All us loved Sharie and worried about her, too, 'cause as white-looking as she was and as pretty as she was, chances were that nothing good was going to come to her.

"She took sick up in the night and by daybreak, she was dead. Didn't nobody even know she was sick, 'cause if they had, they sho' would've got Delilah to heal her. First we knowed anything was the matter was we heard this terrible screaming long 'bout false dawn and looked out to see Sharie's momma running up the quarter hollering for Delilah.

"That night was the burying. It was sad. Back in them days, there never was no time to build a proper coffin for a slave. Just cut a board the shape of your body and tie you on it and lower you down. Lawd, that sho' was a tiny board they tied Sharie on.

"The slave burying ground was on the back edge of the clearing where we had church, and we was standing round the grave out there, holding pine torches to see by, and somebody said a prayer and then we started singing,

> 'Soon one morning,
> Death come a-creeping in my room.
> Soon one morning,
> Death come a-creeping in my room.
> Soon one morning,
> Death come a-creeping in my room.
> Oh, my Lord, oh, my Lord,
> What shall I do?'

And Sharie's momma shrieked and she flung herself at Delilah. 'You can do it, 'Lilah. I knows you can! Please, 'Lilah! Look at my baby! God don't want my baby dead!'

"And a crazy look come in Delilah's eyes, like there was

85

a wind blowing that nobody could feel but her, and she started praying, only this time it was in English, and she was daring God, challenging Him to raise Sharie from the dead and the muscles in her neck were standing out and her eyes were bulging like something was trying to push them out of her head. And Sharie didn't move. Delilah prayed harder and louder, and the peoples started getting restless, like they was embarrassed. Even them what had been going around saying that Delilah had been sent by the Lawd started inching away. I looked around and seen Madame Couseau standing way to one side by herself and it looked to me like she was crying, but my eyes could've been playing tricks on me.

"Delilah prayed until her voice was hoarse and Sharie just lay there and some of the men picked up Sharie's pallet and lowered it down into the grave and Delilah started beating on'em, trying to push'em away, but they didn't pay her no mind, and Simpson started shoveling on the dirt and Sharie's momma tried to jump in the grave but some folks grabbed her and held her and something else snapped in Ora and she started crying and couldn't stop, and then, somebody started that song up again:

> '*I believe that the Lawd has laid His hands on you,*
> *Hands on you, hands on you.*
> *I believe that the Lawd has laid His hands on you,*
> *And that can be a terrible thing.*'

And everybody just drifted away like spirits and went back to the quarters, but wasn't no sleep to be had.

"Didn't nobody come to Delilah for no healing after that. They begun taking their aches and pains back to Madame Couseau like before, but she didn't talk to her remedies in

African no more as she was making them and she didn't sing no more in the night, either.

"Long about planting time that spring, Simpson dug a grave for Delilah right alongside Sharie's and before Christmas, he planted Madame Couseau right next to Delilah. After that we had to depend on the white doctor.

"That ol' slave cemetery probably all growed over now. Then again, if I know Simpson, I wouldn't be surprised if he sneaks out there once every spring and cleans it off. If you want me to, I'll ask him. We didn't have no tombstones back in them days, but I believe I could point right to the place where Delilah is laying right now."

They were silent for a long time. Occasionally Joshua was aware of a dog barking in the distance. Brother Emory got up and came back with two glasses of cool water, and Joshua sipped at his slowly, his eyes staring at but not seeing Brother Emory's vegetable garden and the weed-filled field beyond.

Brother Emory chuckled. "Your daddy was quite a man before his ghosts caught hold to him."

"What do you mean?" Joshua asked quickly, suddenly alert.

"Well, that's what I calls it. He didn't know how to live with his dead, so they took him over. We got to learn to live with the dead as well as the living, you know. But you know that," he said, looking over at Joshua seriously.

Joshua stared back. "I do?"

"Sho'," Brother Emory replied, matter-of-factly. "I knowed that when it was you done the burying of your sister." He chuckled again. "What I just remembered about your father, though, was before that. Used to be a colored evangelist come to town every year around Labor Day. He called hisself a healer and he would hold healing services every night for a week in a tent the white folks would let

87

him pitch in a field on the edge of town. All them po' ignorant colored what live on the Wellington plantation would just flock down to that tent and that man would put his hands on'em, tell'em they was healed, and they would give him all the money they had. That wasn't much, but you put together a lot of little and you got yourself a nice piece of change.

"Well, one year your father went down to the tent meeting every night. Told me, said, 'Brother Emory, that man's a fake and I'm gon' catch him.' Well, I knowed the man was a fake and I sho' wanted to see your poppa catch him. We went every night, sat right up close so's we could see good. Well, on the last night, when that old scalawag claim he took a tumor out of a woman, your poppa marched right up to him, snatched that so-called tumor out of his hands, held it up for everybody to see, and yelled, 'Hog bladder! And I know everybody here know what a hog bladder look like!' And folks started laughing and don't you know, that healing fellow was lucky to get out of town with his life. Folks tore his clothes off looking for their money. Guess you know he ain't been back here since. No other healing fellow either."

Joshua looked at Brother Emory, smiled, and nodded several times, the smile opening his face in the grace of memory restored.

"I believe I could do 'way with a mess of them greens now, Brother Emory. That is, if it wouldn't be too much trouble."

"Son, ain't no more trouble than living is." They laughed.

That evening when Brother Emory took him home, there was a crippled woman he didn't even know waiting in the yard, but before the woman could speak, Brother Emory had sent her on her way. He awoke the next morning afraid that Sister Mary Lou would be there with her husband, Bud, but she wasn't, and by the end of the week, when no one had come to the house asking to be healed, when none of the church members he saw during the week even mentioned what had happened that Sunday morning, he wondered what Brother Emory had said.

He never knew and eventually forgot that once he had made a crippled woman walk. He married, went to seminary in Atlanta while working in a funeral parlor and in a barber shop to support his wife and Louis, who had come to live with them, pastored a country church outside Macon, Georgia, for three years before going to Selma, Alabama, his first church in something that resembled a city.

His ministry was on its way, he'd thought then. No more country churches that couldn't pay enough to live on. No more having to plant a garden, can vegetables, raise chickens, and teach school, build houses, or do something just so he could preach to thirty people every Sunday. He planned to stay in Selma two or three years, keeping his eye open for a church in a bigger city—Mobile, even Birmingham—and then, one day in the next ten years, Chicago, Detroit, St. Louis, and a church so big there would be a hundred people in the choir alone. That wasn't how it turned out, though, and if he had known then that Selma was going to be the biggest place he would ever have a church, he wondered if he would've given up the ministry.

One morning deep in the summer of his only year in Selma he was sitting on the porch of Brother Willie McGhee and his wife. They were two of the oldest members of the church and very influential. His success in Selma depended on their opinion, and at least once a week, he stopped by just to talk.

He couldn't remember what they were talking about that particular morning, but he was sure he had nodded his head in apparent agreement as he stared at the few people going along the street.

He wondered if they'd paved the streets in the colored

section of Selma yet. They hadn't back when King had that march there, he knew, because he'd seen it on television. King talking about getting colored the vote when he should've been trying to get the streets paved so a person wouldn't have to sit on the porch in the summer with the dust of the road blowing in their house, or having their cars and wagons mired in the mud in the winter and spring.

A tall woman, thin as a wisp of wind and tall as hope, walked past the house, slowed, turned and came back, then walked up to the house. Her skin was the soft black of a gentle death, and her head was swathed with a wrapping made from a flour sack. She wore a shiny red sleeveless dress cut too low in front for a proper Christian woman. The dress was dirty, but it clung tightly to the curves of her slender body and full bosom, so tightly that Reverend Smith could see that no underclothes intervened between dress and body.

She walked up the steps to the porch, stopping before the last step, and stared at him. "Somebody said you the preacher," she announced belligerently, one hand on her hip.

"I'm Reverend Joshua Smith of Temple Mission Baptist Church."

"Is you a Christian preacher?" she asked in the same challenging tone, reaching inside her unsheathed bosom to pull out a floppy cigarette stained with sweat.

"All preachers are Christian," he answered sententiously.

"Shit! Don't give me that. Nigger preachers ain't no better than a dog in heat."

"You watch how you talk around the Reverend," Brother McGhee said hotly, getting out of his rocking chair. "You get on away from here. Don't want your kind on my porch."

"Sit your little bony ass down before I sit it down for you! This don't concern you, old man!" She lit the cigarette and through the smoke curling from its tip, squinted at Brother McGhee as he struggled for a dignified retreat.

"You want me to send for the high sheriff?" he asked Reverend Smith, easing back into his chair.

"That won't be necessary," Reverend Smith said simply.

The woman looked at him and nodded. "Folks said you was different. Said you cares about the po' peoples."

"Different and too good for somebody like you," Sister McGhee put in.

The woman didn't even favor her with a glance, but gazed at Reverend Smith, who met and held the gaze.

Once, not too many years ago, she had been beautiful, he thought. Even now her large eyes had a languid enchantment, and when she was younger, they must have carried a limpid and teasing sensuality.

"What can I do for you?" he asked.

"It ain't me, Reverend." Her voice was softer now. "It's my baby. I know I don't look like much and these folks here are right. Somebody like me ain't got no right to come and take up your time. But I heard different ones in town talk about you. Say you the best-dressed colored man in Selma, and that include the bootleggers and the gamblers. So when I was coming from town a little while ago and seen this well-dressed, dignified man, I figured it must be you." She took the cigarette from her mouth and started to drop it on the porch, changed her mind, and flicked it into the road with a well-practiced thumb and forefinger. "My little girl—Marie—she 'leven months—she sick and I done sent for the white doctor every day but he ain't come and I reckon he won't. I was just hoping you would come and say a few words of prayer." She looked down at her dusty bare feet.

"Where do you live?"

"Round yonder," she said quickly, looking up and pointing down the street. "Just go up to the corner and turn left. Ain't no numbers on the houses. Mines is about three-quarters way down on the right-hand side. Looks like a store. I be waiting out front for you. I wouldn't want nobody to see you walking along the street with me. You a good man. Got a pretty wife, I hear. And these niggers in this town got tongues like razors. They'd talk you out of town if you was seen walking with somebody like me."

"I'll be there directly."

She smiled then, and it was a shy smile of unaccustomed gratitude.

"Reverend, we can't let you go around there," Brother McGhee said before she was scarcely off the porch. "Every cutthroat and backslider in Selma lives down that alley."

"It's a trick," Sister McGhee added vehemently. "I'll bet my life that there's a passel of cutthroats waiting at her house to take everything you got."

The thought had occurred to him, but he wouldn't admit it aloud. "Well, if Jesus could walk among people like that, I don't suppose I can do less."

"You a good Christian, Reverend," Sister McGhee said. "Maybe too good."

He chuckled. "That's not possible, Sister McGhee."

"Well, Reverend. I don't mean to be sticking my nose in your business, but you ain't Jesus, you know. And you young. You ain't been a preacher too long. You don't know the niggers of this world the way I do. Now, when you come here to be interviewed, I could see that you was a young man on the rise and our church wasn't nothing but a stepping-stone for you, but that was all right. I'd be proud to be able to say I knew you when, and hope that when you had a big church in Detroit or Chicago, you'd remember us down here and come back once a year and let us hear you preach." Brother McGhee paused. "But this church

can also be a stepping-stone down. You understand what
I'm saying?"

Reverend Smith stood up slowly. "You wouldn't be
threatening me, would you, Brother McGhee?"

"Just telling you the facts, young fella. You can go on
down to that tramp's house if you want to, thinking you
Jesus, but I ain't never seen Jesus put no groceries on
nobody's dinner table. All I know is that we don't want our
pastor consorting with women like that."

Reverend Smith put on his straw hat, and he wasn't
surprised then or now by what he said, because it needed
saying. "Brother McGhee," he began quietly, "you can
kiss my black ass."

As he turned down the street she'd indicated, it was
evident that the McGhees were right about one thing: It
was an alley, a narrow lane of two deep ruts on either side
of a narrow strip of weeds. Only someone of infinite tact
and kindness would've called the buildings lining both sides
houses, and a self-respecting farmer would have protested
at keeping his mule or storing tools in any one of them.
The shacks had wooden shutters instead of windows and
Reverend Smith remembered houses like that in Ouichitta.
"Them's from slavery times," Poppa had told him.

He walked slowly along the narrow middle strip, knowing
how foolish he looked in his white suit, shirt, and black
tie, black-and-white shoes, and hard straw hat with the
round brim. People sat as still as the heat on porches and
steps, on boxes turned on end, in rickety chairs, old, young,
middle-aged, all barefooted. He heard a dog growl men-
acingly from the porch of a shack where a woman sat on
the step, a baby asleep at her dust-brown breast. Without
taking her dull eyes from him, she slapped the dog on the
nose with her fist. It howled and slinked off the porch to
crawl beneath the house.

He was more than halfway down the alley before he saw a building whose sides were covered with metal signs advertising Royal Crown Cola, Nehi Grape, and Silvercup Bread. She stood in the road and was waving at him. She had changed dresses and was wearing a flower print dress with sleeves. Her hair was combed and brushed now.

"I didn't believe sho' 'nuf that you would come."

"Well, you look more like the pretty girl you are," he said, smiling back at her.

"Thank you, Reverend," and as dark-skinned as she was, he knew she was blushing.

"Where's the baby?"

"She in the house. You go on in and 'scuse the way it look. I be out here. If I go in with you, it'll be all over town by nightfall."

It took a moment for his eyes to adjust to the darkness inside. There was only the one room with a small fireplace where a cast-iron pot hung from a hook. He understood now why one side of the house was covered by the metal store signs, because they covered large holes where boards were rotted away. In the close heat of the room, the air smelled of sweat and odors he did not care to name. In a back corner, a naked child lay on a thin, ripped mattress, immobile as a doll among the weeds of a junk-strewn vacant lot.

He stared at her. Her body twitched fitfully and she moaned as her tiny hands brushed at the flies crawling over the sores on her legs and body.

He looked around the room despairingly. The red dress hung on a nail next to the door with a few other pieces of cloth that had been clothes once, and he wondered if she wore no underclothes because she had none. There was no table or chair in the room, no food, no pictures on the wall. A tin plate, a fork in it, sat on the hearth before the fireplace.

What was he supposed to do at the center of such emptiness? Pray? Pray that the baby on the filthy mattress would die so she wouldn't grow up to sit on a porch and stare with eyes as lifeless as dead bees? Or would he curse God for allowing a baby to be born for no reason other than to provide pus for garbage-eating flies?

That girl waiting outside wouldn't know any difference if he left now. She was grateful that he had come and she certainly couldn't think that his being there could make any difference. Yet, she had gone out of her way to see him. Did she have more faith in him as a man of God than he did?

The baby was crying. He went over to the mattress and knelt reluctantly. "Now, now," he whispered, taking off his straw hat and fanning her. She was a fat little baby, bloated into a charade of health by malnutrition. He put his free hand on her forehead and the heat that burned it was not of the fetid air but from within her body. Myra and Sue Ann had been hot like that.

He picked her up and rocked her in the cradle of his arm. Her crying subsided and she looked up at him with wide and blank eyes. He stared back and tears flooded his eyes, surprising him, and before he could wonder how or why, a cold shiver rippled through his body and he was remembering the Monday morning after the Sunday he had healed Sister Adams and how he had gotten up early, before the dipper moon slipped beneath the firmament, and carrying a hoe, ridden a mule up to the ridge behind the house and gone down to the cemetery on the hillside. It was a job he had been thinking about for several weeks and he wanted to get it over with before the heat of the day.

He worked quickly, the sharp edge of the hoe pulling the grasses and weeds out by their roots, which he pushed over beside the fence where they made an unintentional and scraggly border. One summer soon he wouldn't be there to weed, and what then? It wouldn't take more than a year or two for the cemetery to disappear beneath the weeds and grasses. And what then?

That was how it was going to be, and there wasn't a thing he could do about it just as he hadn't been able to do anything about Myra or Sue Ann and what good was it to have healing power if he hadn't known nothing about it until after Sue Ann and Myra were dead and he leaned against the hoe, tears coursing down his face in sorrow and anger, and now, holding that black, dirty feverish baby in his arms, the tears came again and he pressed the child against his chest, unmindful of his pristine white suit and told God, "You owe me this one!," though afterward he would have little memory of having dared to so address God, or that he had walked back and forth, back and forth across the floor of the tiny room for more than an hour, trying to make God do his will, and finally, his steps slowed and he awakened to that fatigue he had known once before, that weight so heavy that he wanted only to curl up inside his body.

He lay the baby gently on the dirty mattress and she stirred for a moment before sinking back into the cleanness of sleep. Reverend Smith got up and wiped his eyes. He blinked slowly and the shabby room came back into focus.

Lethargically he went onto the porch.

"You was in there so long," she said anxiously, getting up from the top step. "Is-is—," but she couldn't finish.

He squinted against the relentless heat and light, but his body was trembling, and she, whose name he realized he did not know, noticed.

"You shivering like it's wintertime," she said, and moved as if to take his hands between hers and rub warmth into them, but he waved her away with a weary brusqueness.

"She'll be all right now," he heard himself say in a disembodied voice. "And if anybody asks about the baby, you just tell them she got better. You hear? Don't tell them nothing else! You understand me?"

She nodded, frightened by the anger in his voice.

"And you straighten up your life and come to church sometime and thank God for what He did for you in there!"

She nodded eagerly. "Yes, sir. Yes, sir. I sho' will."

He stumbled off the porch and up the alley like a drunkard, knowing he would never see her again.

Late the following spring, two weeks before he was to leave to go to his new church in Bayou Bottom, Louisiana, he looked out over the congregation and saw her and the little girl sitting on the back row, both in long pretty white dresses. She waited for him after church.

"Remember me?" she asked shyly.

"Yes, I do," he told her. "Never did know your name, though."

"I was too 'shamed to give it. Nora. Nora Mae."

"Well, Nora. You seem to be doing all right for yourself."

She grinned. "I wanted to come to church before now, but I didn't want to come in looking like a dustrag. I got a job cooking for a white lady. I lives on the place, 'cause I told the lady I wasn't gon' leave my baby all by herself every day. So she lets me stay there with the baby and I cooks and cleans."

"That's nice." He stooped down and smiled at the girl. She hid behind her mother's dress and peeked out with one eye. "Hello, Marie."

"You remember her name?" Nora asked, amazed.

He put his index finger out toward Marie, and after a pause, she grabbed it and giggled.

"Well, now, that's a fine young lady," he chuckled. He

shook her hand. "How do you do? I'm so pleased to meet you."

Every year he received a Christmas card from Nora. She'd eventually managed to save enough money to go to a cosmetology school and after some years of scrimping and saving, had opened her own beauty parlor in Selma. He remembered sending Marie a present when she graduated from high school.

He stepped onto the lawn to look closely at the house. It was made of gray fieldstone, solid and undistinguished on a block of similar houses on a nondescript street in Nashville, Tennessee. Thirty years ago it looked unlike any other house on the block, because it was going to be his. After twenty-five years of living in parsonages and rented houses, they were buying a home. Until he signed the papers he hadn't been sure the old white woman was going to sell, though. Somewhere in the file cabinet in his study, there was the deed with the paragraph in it forbidding a sale to "a colored person or Jew."

Reverend Smith didn't know what made her sell to him, or what made him decide to be the first colored on the block, knowing that a cross might be burned on his lawn, or a bomb thrown through a window one night.

He made his way across the lawn and down the driveway to the back of the house. He stood for a moment in the shadow of the empty garage and stared at the house. A new roof had been put on two years ago and the gutters were replaced last year. There were no cracks or crevices in the foundation. The railing on the back stairs could use a little strengthening, though, and the screen door replacing.

It was cooler with the shade of morning over the yard. He stood erect, his hand resting lightly for support on the curved handle of the wooden cane. His gaze moved slowly over the garage, where the basketball hoop he'd put up for Carl was still attached, rusted to granules of dark brown like his own life. He turned and stared at the wide strip of earth beside the garage, where no flowers bloomed this year. He didn't have to walk behind the garage to see the weeds growing where vegetables should've been.

He missed digging in the earth. It was the one thing he'd done longer than he'd preached. As a boy he'd looked forward to going to the field, his hoe over his shoulder, and as an older boy, to hitching the mule to the plow.

I will lift up mine eyes unto the hills, from whence cometh my help. Neither of his sons knew what it was to stand alone in the middle of a field, leaning on a hoe and looking up to see hills like lambs against the sky. But how could they? He had moved away from all that before they were born. How could he blame them for not knowing what he hadn't given them the opportunity to learn? Had he ever asked them to place a seed in a furrow? Had he put their hands on a tomato plant and guided them in removing the suckers? And why hadn't he, if he wanted so desperately now to know there was something tangible of him that would remain?

There was a sudden tightening in his chest and he gripped the cane tightly to keep from falling. The pain subsided quickly, but he was breathing heavily, afraid to move, afraid to learn that he had died.

He began humming to himself, as he had done ever since the heart attack when he needed to know that he was still alive. His voice was all remaining that had not betrayed him.

It was the voice that made a preacher a preacher rather than a minister. Anybody who liked people, had common sense and a Bible could be a minister, but a preacher was all that plus the voice. Even when he was little, the old folks had said, "He's gon' be a preacher. Listen at that voice." He thought everybody knew how to let their voices be as soft as sunlight in spring and as hot as railroad tracks against bare feet in August. As he got older and listened to preachers, he realized that most shouted and yelled, trying to cover up that they didn't have the voice. Others didn't even pretend, but read their sermons like college professors giving lectures.

Sometimes his voice was an arrow in silent, pointed flight; other times it was like a lasso which caught and held souls, pulling them into his; it could be a sledgehammer, too, shattering and pulverizing the strong and the proud.

As he hummed to himself he remembered standing in the pulpit of a thousand thousand churches and in the middle of a sermon his big, deep voice surprising him with a song. It was like a rushing wind filling every corner of the church and if the pianist or organist dared to accompany him, the voice increased in size until the piano or organ could not be heard and the church windows rattled in their frames. As the voices of the congregation joined the song, his became an ark in which theirs rode. That was why he became known as the "Singing Evangelist."

Listening to his voice, he walked slowly up the back steps and into the house. Beads of perspiration like pimples stood on his forehead. She'd been right. His days of being in the sun were past.

He walked through the empty kitchen and not seeing her, assumed she was in the bedroom making the beds. He went into the living room where he sat down wearily in his leather recliner and was asleep, it seemed, before his eyes closed. But there was no clean separation between sleep and wakefulness any longer. Now that he was barred from the future, images of the past were freed from memory's prison and floated unbidden to the surface of his mind like corpses from undiscovered shipwrecks on the ocean's bottom. He watched them come, the faces, rooms, churches, highways, and he did not know if he was asleep and dreaming, or awake and remembering, or if each was the other and both one.

Since the stroke he had begun walking across the landscape of the past and the more he walked, the further away its horizon. The past seemed larger now than the future had appeared when he was young and possibility was all and the world was all possibility, even for one as black as him.

Why was the realm of the past vaster than future's sphere had been ever? Was it because possibility was an illusion of youth, while the past (when one had earned it) was like the curved dome of night into which he gazed in wonder and with awe? The past was an actuality whose detail and reality could not be seen and examined when it was present. Only now, when there was nothing but past, did it surface to be examined and lived truly for the first time. When past was all, present was all, and there were no uncertainties and anxieties because the resolution was known.

He looked at the photograph of his two sons on the console television set diagonally across from him, his head slumped on his chest, his lips parted as if he were in a drunken slumber. Josh was always seventeen in the frame on the television, poised on the brink of manhood, a cocky assurance in his eyes and the slight upturn of the lips. What had happened to this firstborn namesake who ambled into his hospital room last summer, a tiny gray straw hat on his head, the top three buttons of his pink shirt undone so that the silver-filled chains around his neck glistened against his brown chest like the foil from old cigarette packs on a deserted picnic ground. His face was drawn tight as if something within had eaten the life. He looked like an aged and aging man to whom youth was clinging like a putrefying corpse. He looked so much like Dallas that Reverend Smith had been momentarily confused, afraid that the stroke had affected his mind.

It wasn't Dallas, and yet, it was and had been that day in late May three months after he had so proudly taken his sons to the photographer and maybe Josh had known, which was why he stared into the camera lens with the confidence of one who held a secret that, when released, would change irrevocably what was and would be. He came into the house on the last day of his high-school life, some papers folded in his hand. Without a hello or any prelude, he thrust them at his father: "Sign'em! I want to get the hell out of this house as quick as I can!" He went to the kitchen where he hugged and kissed his mother, opened the refrigerator, and took out a cold leg of fried chicken and began gnawing on it. Reverend Smith unfolded the papers: They were enlistment forms for the army, already filled out, with a red X on the line where he was to sign giving his seventeen-year-old underage son permission.

Now that all was past and past all, he acknowledged that Josh's eagerness to leave had been his, also. When all was present, or appeared so, he had been trapped in the conventions of emotions, and dutifully felt the hurt, loss, sense of failure, and anger, not knowing that these were like layers of varnish on a piece of furniture under which hid a rich oaken slab of wood.

She still faulted him. "You were too hard on Josh and too easy on Carl. Anything Josh ever wanted, you told him he couldn't have, but everything Carl said he wanted, you couldn't wait to get in the car and go to town to get." She didn't understand and he never explained about that long, loose-limbed walk. It wasn't a father's job to love his sons like a mother did, but to stand apart and see into them.

It was another way of loving, and it looked hard and harsh if you didn't know what it took to be a man in the world. So he had ignored her when he used his belt on Josh and ignored her when he opened a charge account at a bookstore for Carl when he was only fourteen. And he waited.

He waited from the day he drove Josh to the bus station to go to basic training. "You not gon' beat my butt any-more," he fumed as Reverend Smith guided the car through the light afternoon traffic. "Uh-uh! I must've been crazy to let you do that, me six-foot-one and you five-seven standing on your tiptoes. And I'll tell you something else! Every Sunday morning at eleven o'clock when you stand up in the pulpit to start church, you can know for a fact that I'll be laying up drunk somewhere. You hear me? So you'll never have to wonder what church I'm in on Sunday mornings. I'm declaring my membership right now in the Church of Good Times. Easy money, easy women, and easy living is my religion, and may I live forever!"

Reverend Smith listened, amazed that Josh had the voice, too, but didn't know it.

"And while I'm at it, let me tell you something else. You think you such a good Christian and I know you're convinced that if anybody is going to Heaven, you are. Maybe that's why I'm going to do everything I know how to make sure I go to Hell, because if you're going to be in Heaven, I don't want to be there. But I really shouldn't worry about that, because I won't even raise an eyebrow when I get to Hell and see you there as gatekeeper."

Reverend Smith said nothing until it was almost time for the bus to leave. Then he looked up at his older son, who stared over his head and into some angry beyond. "You're going to be disappointed when you find out that you are more my son this way than if you had done everything I wanted you to do." He walked away and waited.

He waited through the years when Josh addressed his

letters only to Carlotta, through the furloughs home when he said as few words as possible to his father. When Josh wrote him, it was only to ask for money without a word as to why it was needed. Reverend Smith sent it, time after time, acknowledging this ritual of revenge which extracted no blood.

It was late in the winter of 1962 when Ol' Lady Daniels died. Ninety-three years she lived on the place where she had been born. She had long ago changed her initial impression of him and his color. He knew from the way she smiled at him each time he and Carlotta visited, from the way she kept the little bottles of perfume he brought her, kept them unopened and unused on her dresser. He had paid to have electricity put in her house and would've paid for indoor plumbing but she said she couldn't live under the same roof with a bathroom, that it seemed downright nasty to shit where you lived. Even if he was a preacher, Ol' Lady Daniels's vocabulary remained the same, limited and expressive.

She was perhaps as close as he had had to a mother, not one to whom he could talk his heart's wonderings but a mother to whom he could offer the gratitude for being. She accepted that summer night sitting on the porch with him and Carlotta, the two of them swaying gently back and forth in the same porch swing in which they'd courted, as she rocked energetically in her rocking chair.

"Joshua!" she said suddenly. "I want you to preach my funeral when my time comes. Don't want none of these damned young preachers doing it. You get closer to God when you fart than they do in a year of what they call preaching. And don't nobody know me like you do. Don't want no long-drawn-out sad funeral. Ain't no goddam reason why anybody should be sorry when somebody old as me die. I'm seventy-seven and anybody live that long is stealing somebody else's time anyway. So I don't want nobody leaving my funeral feeling sad, 'cause you better goddam well believe that I ain't gon' be feeling sad lying in that box."

He'd never liked winter funerals. It was hard enough getting through winter without death, too. If the funeral was late over in the winter, it meant that the frost would be in the ground and the gravedigger would have to use a pickax to dig the grave and depending on how long it took him, the funeral could be delayed for days.

He awoke to the sound of rain the morning of her funeral and knew that she wouldn't get her wish for a happy funeral. The only thing worse than a winter funeral was one in the rain. Even at funerals where everybody in the church agreed that the deceased fully merited his timely death, a wife who had sent her husband into the beyond with a knife-thrust to the heart cried tears matching in volume the rain outside. He had not expected either to see Josh coming down the road through the rain as they got ready to go to the church.

"Momma called me," he said, "and I got the first plane out of Chicago. Took the bus from Little Rock and talked the driver into coming down this far and letting me off."

Reverend Smith wanted to know if Carl was coming. Josh didn't know. Carlotta said he wasn't. She hadn't called him.

At the cemetery after the funeral, he was glad Josh was there, because Carlotta stared down into the grave which filled with water quicker than the gravedigger could keep it bailed and when the casket was lowered into it, the displaced water rising up its sides and lapping at the top, Carlotta screamed and unleashed screaming from all sides of the grave. Never had he to call on his voice to be so powerful, to contain and surround the mourning until the weeping and sobbing, the screaming and crying were held tenderly within his voice:

"Jesus said, I am the resurrection and the life." His voice did not become louder, but bigger, as if it were a large cathedral bell whose solemn tolling was the heartbeat of a waning moon. "He that believeth in me, though he were dead, yet shall he live." He did not shout above the screaming, but lowered his voice so that it became the foundation on which the screams settled like crows on a gnarled and naked limb. "And whosoever liveth and believeth in me shall never die." He motioned for the gravedigger to start filling in the grave, quickly, to shovel in enough dirt to absorb the water. "He shall feed his flock like a shepherd: He shall gather the lambs with his arm, and carry them in His bosom," and then his voice found one of the old songs. It was a dangerous song, because it could push the mourners and his wife into irretrievable hysteria but he trusted the voice:

Soon one morning death come a-creeping in my room.
Soon one morning death come a-creeping in my room.
Soon one morning death come a-creeping in my room.
Oh, my Lord! Oh, my Lord!
What shall I do?

And many of the old people at the graveside remembered and sang, and their voices, veined with age and suffering, gave the mourning form and the grief content and he led them away from the grave, a solemn recessional of mortality.

Soon one morning death come a-creeping in my room.
Soon one morning death come a-creeping in my room.
Soon one morning death come a-creeping in my room.

Oh, my Lord! Oh, my Lord!
What will I do?

Josh held his mother tightly and helped her into the backseat of the black funeral limousine as the rain of late winter slid down her face as if it were a pane of glass.

Once back at the house the mourners didn't stay long, though it was the first time any of them had been inside. Even dead, Ol' Lady Daniels made them feel like trespassers. They chatted briefly with Reverend Smith, expressing their condolences, and departed, leaving platters of fried chicken, ham, biscuits, sweet potatoes, greens, pies, cakes, and bottles of Coca-Cola.

When the last ones left, and it seemed that no more would come, Reverend Smith went into the front room and saw Josh kneeling beside the bed, a pan of water next to him, applying compresses to his mother's head.

"I don't think she's going to get any rest, Daddy, without a sedative or something," he said, turning halfway to look at his father beseechingly.

"She should have some pills in her purse," Reverend Smith said.

"She already took a couple of those and they don't seem to be doing any good."

Reverend Smith's shoulders slumped as he thought about having to go into the rain again. "I'll go over to the house next door and call Doctor Mimms," he said wearily.

Turning to leave the room, her angry voice stopped him. "I don't see why you wanted to sing that old-timey, mournful song. That just made everything worse, and it was bad enough already!"

He whirled around to say something he knew would be better left unsaid, and as he opened his mouth to say it, she sobbed violently and seized Josh's hand and squeezed it tightly. Josh put an arm around her, whispering, "Now, mother. Everything's going to be all right."

Reverend Smith stared intently at them for a moment, then took a deep breath, let it out slowly, and went into the rain. It pounded on him, making his clothes heavy and cold again as he walked across the yard to the house that stood in what had been the orchard once. The hundred acres Ol' Lady Daniels owned when he'd first come there had been sold, piece by piece, during the last twenty years as age made it difficult and then impossible for her to work the place anymore. Ten acres remained, and they would be sold now, if Carlotta let him.

After phoning the colored doctor, he started wearily back to the house, and the walk through the relentless rain seemed like an act of atonement. Not for sin, but for how things were, and had to be, it seemed, given that he and she were only human.

He stopped and raised his face to the rain and it struck, stinging-needle-cold and he flinched at the tiny pains, wanting to cry because truth was as ugly as death as being lowered into a water-filled grave and salvation was learning, again and again, not to deny the need for salvation.

He didn't know how many funerals he had preached in the past thirty-eight years. Five hundred. A thousand?—babies so tiny they looked like dolls; soldiers brought home in flag-draped caskets from the battlefields of France, Germany, Italy, and Korea, some of them young men he had baptized when they were no longer than their mother's forearms; young brides; husbands who had finally gotten the jobs that would've let them support their families with ease; the old who had been looking forward to the years of sleeping late in the mornings and going to the ball park in the afternoons; the murdered, the burned, the suicides; the broken, mangled, and smashed pried from wrecked cars.

Most funerals left a chalky aftertaste because between deceased and survivors there was always too much that had been left unsaid and undone, because they had thought there would always be time. God did not guarantee tomorrow, however. He didn't even promise the next minute as the second hand swept past the thirty-second mark.

He didn't want it to be that way with him and Carlotta, with him and Josh, and he didn't know how it could be otherwise, but atonement was the one act of love that really mattered, wasn't it?

He lowered his head and walked on the porch, standing there for a moment to let the water run off his clothes before going into Ol' Lady Daniels's bedroom and stripping. He would've liked nothing more than to take a hot shower or bath, but in a house without plumbing, that wasn't going to be possible. So he rubbed his body vigorously with a thick green towel before putting on dry clothes.

He picked up the heavy, soggy pile of wet clothes and went down the corridor to the back porch where he flung them over the railing beside Josh's. He hurried back inside out of the driving rain and lay down on the bed and was almost asleep when he heard Josh open the front door and let in the doctor.

Reverend Smith got up and started across the room, then stopped, as he heard the door to the bedroom across the hall close. He went back and sat on the side of the bed.

He ran his hand slowly over the quilt Ol' Lady Daniels had made before he was born probably, the quilt on which his wife had been born. He would've much preferred to sleep in a motel or hotel, but Pine Grove didn't have one for colored. So he would sleep in the bed of his wife's birth and his mother-in-law's death and hope neither had left any dreams or nightmares for him.

When he heard the doctor leave, he went down the hallway and into the dining room, which was also the living room and workroom and even bathroom, because on Saturday nights, the round galvanized tub had been taken down from its nail on the back porch and placed next to the wood stove in the far corner of the room. He had given Josh and Carl many baths in that tub, pouring two or three inches of hot water in it from the cast-iron kettle on the stove and an inch or so of cold from the pail of water that was always in the kitchen.

He went over to the stove, took some newspaper and kindling from the box next to it, kindling split when he and Carlotta had come to visit at Christmas. He got a few small logs from the woodbox in the kitchen, laid them neatly on the kindling, and quickly had a fire going.

Standing with his back to the stove, he looked idly around the room while the increasing warmth took the last of the day's chill from his body. Beneath the glare of the naked light bulb hanging from the ceiling over the table, the room looked worn and weary. Perhaps it had looked so for the last twenty years, but in the glow of a kerosene lamp on the table, he had been aware only of a circle of yellow light inside which he sat with a comforting darkness surrounding him. Such a darkness had surrounded him thirty-eight years ago on a Saturday night in July when he asked Carlotta to marry him. The wallpaper had been white then. Now it was yellowed and browned like a bouquet of chrysanthemums, and in places, had rolled away from the wall in large torn strips.

He remembered offering numerous times to repaper the room.

"What an ol' lady like me care about wallpaper, Joshua? Didn't care about such when I was young. Damned if I'm going to start now."

He had laughed then and he smiled now, taking a step

away from the rapidly heating stove. Since he'd been a man, she was the only person who'd called him Joshua. Everybody else called him Reverend Smith, even Carlotta. Thirty-eight years of getting up and laying down together and he had never heard his first name pass her lips.

"You don't have to call me 'Reverend Smith,' you know," he'd told her during that awful first year of their marriage.

"I know," she agreed pleasantly. "But that's who you were to me when I met you, and calling you anything else wouldn't feel right."

Ol' Lady Daniels called him "Reverend Smith" in public, but there, at the place, he was just Joshua. He was going to miss her. He was going to miss this house, too. Not the house as a building, but the memories of himself as much a part of it now as the nails and knotholes he could see where the wallpaper had peeled away. How do you live with your dead, he suddenly wanted to ask Brother Emory, long dead himself, when your dead take something of you into the grave with them and the older you are and the older they are, the more of you they take.

There was the sound of movement from the front room and he looked up to see Josh, closing the door behind him, exhaling with a long, silent aspiration.

"She's finally asleep," he said softly. "She should sleep through the night. The doctor gave me a prescription and I'll get up first thing in the morning and go to town and get it filled."

He came over to the stove and Reverend Smith moved to one side to make room for him.

"This fire sure feels good," Josh said self-consciously.

"I see you got out of your wet clothes," Reverend Smith offered tentatively, aware suddenly that he was alone with his firstborn son for the first time in fifteen years. He felt intimidated by the six inches more in height Josh carried and the ease with which he stood in his tall body, as if there were no cares or sorrows that would do more than make him pause in his dance through life.

"I got a chance to change right after we got back from the cemetery while some of the women were getting Momma into dry clothes. When I get to heaven, I'm sure gon' give Grandmomma a bill for that suit," he laughed. "Of course, that's assuming she made it up there."

Reverend Smith chuckled. "And that's assuming you get up there."

"You ain't just whistling 'Dixie' on that one," Josh agreed, and he and his father laughed together.

"What did the doctor say?" Reverend Smith wanted to know.

"Not much. I told him that we'd just come from burying her mother. He just nodded, reached in his bag and pulled out the longest needle I've ever seen, filled it with something, and shot it in her arm. Gave me the prescription, asked for ten dollars, and was gone."

"My billfold's in the other room," Reverend Smith put in quickly. "I'll reimburse you."

"Now, I know the polite thing to do is to refuse it. However, there is also such a thing as being too polite, and you wouldn't want me to overdo it, would you?"

They laughed loudly, too loudly and an instant longer than the joking merited, but they recognized, with a tentative surprise, that perhaps they could now expose their differences in the truth of humor rather than behead each other with truth's sharp edges.

"You hungry?" Reverend Smith asked.

"I was just looking at all that food on the table."

"Wait'll you go back in the kitchen. There's twice as much back there."

"I bet there ain't a chicken left alive in the state of

Arkansas." Josh shook his head. "I don't see why these people would waste all this food on the three of us, especially when a lot of them can hardly afford to put a decent meal on their own tables."

"That ain't the point. It's their way of saying they know and they care."

"If you say so."

Reverend Smith recognized the curt tone of dismissal and fifteen years ago he would've taken his belt off automatically or told Josh not to talk to him in that tone of voice. It hadn't worked then and it was a foolish thing to remember now.

The darkness of the day had given way to night, and the rain intensified suddenly until it sounded like a crew of carpenters pounding nails into the roof.

"Wouldn't you know Grandmomma would pick a day like this to be buried?"

"What do you mean?"

Josh shrugged. "You know how she was. If there was an easy way to do something, she wouldn't take it." He shook his head. "I used to hate to see summer come, because we had to come down here for a month. Nobody to play with, 'cause she wouldn't let anybody in the yard. No electricity, so you couldn't even listen to the radio. Nothing to do except feed the chickens and chop her kindling wood for the winter. And nobody to talk to, 'cause Grandmomma was not the kind like you read about in books who bake cookies for their grandchildren and tell them fairy tales. I don't think in all the years I had to come down here that she ever said more than, 'Hello, boy,' 'Go bring me a bucket of water, boy,' and 'Good-bye, boy,' when it was time for us to go. I never figured out what that white-looking lady had to do with me."

Reverend Smith stepped over to the table and got a

chicken thigh. "This chicken was fried by Sister Franklin and anybody in Pine Grove will tell you that her fried chicken is the best in America."

"Well, maybe I just better put that to the test," Josh said with a chuckle, going over to the table.

"Your grandmother wasn't easy to know," Reverend Smith said, between chewing.

"Did anybody really know her, except Momma?"

"I believe I did." He paused, then nodded. "I know I did," he said with a certainty he would not have had if she were still alive.

"Really?"

Reverend Smith wondered if he detected a touch of sarcasm in Josh's voice and glanced up to see an open curiosity on his face.

"Wasn't easy. It just took her a while to get used to somebody, and the problem was that unless you married into the family, you were never around her long enough for her to get used to you. And, you had to understand her," he added, gratified to know that he now had the words for the understanding.

Josh chuckled. "Well, please explain her to me."

"I remember one time we came down to spend a week late in the fall. We did that every year after she started getting up in years and wasn't able to do as much. Carl and I would help her get the cotton ginned, baled, and sold, help her slaughter the hogs and put up the meat for curing and get her wood in for the winter. Well, this particular year we were sitting around that table there. She got to talking about a bull she wanted to buy and using him for breeding purposes and wanted to know what I thought, and we talked the thing over, back and forth, until she decided not to do it. But she knew more about dairy farming than I did and she knew she did. Suddenly, she laughed, 'I woulda been something if I'd been a man, wouldn't I have, Joshua?' I laughed, said, 'Sister Daniels, God knew that the world wasn't ready for you as a man.' And she thought that was the funniest thing she'd ever heard. It became like a joke between us. But that was the key to her, I think. 'Cause her husband died when she was so young, she had to become a man to make it and she'd found that it was to her liking."

"Did she ever talk to you about Granddaddy? What he was like or anything?"

Reverend Smith opened the stove door and threw the chicken bone in. "No, she didn't. Never told your mother anything either, not even his name."

"That don't make sense," Josh protested.

"Well, I think she totally forgot him."

Josh shook his head. "Don't make sense to me. Any napkins in the kitchen?"

"Should be some in there somewhere."

Josh returned a minute later with paper napkins and two plates and silverware. "I don't know about you, but I think it's time to do some serious eating. Maybe these country Negroes knew what they were doing bringing all this food," he laughed.

They sat down at the table and filled their plates with chicken, ham, greens, and biscuits.

"Don't get me wrong," Josh said, resuming the previous conversation. "I liked her, but just never felt like I knew her. Seems like she got on better with Carl. They'd feed the chickens together and he'd even take her out in the field driving one of them mules and he couldn't been no more than seven at the time, because he was only eight when I joined the army."

"Well, he took an interest in what interested her. So, I guess it was natural that she'd talk to him."

Josh chuckled. "You got a point there. I wasn't about to learn how to drive a mule or do nothing else on this farm. I must've been born with big city in my blood. Neon lights. Smog, traffic. Noise. Ain't nothing on a farm that's natural as far as I'm concerned."

"She knew that's how you felt."

"Huh?" Josh said, surprised.

"I don't remember when it was, but it was probably the last summer or the next to last one we made you come. But you were old enough to walk into town by yourself, and you'd be gone first thing in the morning, and I don't think we should talk about when you'd get back."

Josh sat back in his chair and laughed. "Oh, yes! I remember that summer. Only summer I ever enjoyed down here. That was the last one. I was sixteen. Oh, yes!"

Reverend Smith smiled. "You had that much fun, huh?" he teased.

"Daddy, I don't think you want to know."

"I suspect I don't," he chuckled. "Well, anyway, your grandmomma said, 'Joshua.' You remember how she talked. Deep voice and she talked fast and choppy like. 'Joshua. You can forget about that boy being a preacher.' "

Josh laughed until he was almost out of breath. "Did she really say that?"

"Sure as I'm sitting here."

"And what did you say when she said that?" Josh asked with too much heartiness.

"Said, 'Sister Daniels, I'll be happy if somebody doesn't knife him or shoot him before he's twenty-one.' And she said, 'Don't worry. He laugh too much to get in deep trouble.' "

Josh exploded into another paroxysm of laughter, laughing until the tears rolled down his face.

"I'm sure sorry I never got to know her. I sure am."

With memory and loss as a bond, they settled into the intimacy of eating. From time to time Reverend Smith glanced covertly at Josh, amazed that his appetite had not abated over the years. He had never known anyone who could put away so much food. He smiled to himself. It was silly the kinds of things fathers took pride in, even if it had nothing to do with them. But was it the same for sons? Did this son swell inside with a sense of proprietorship about him?

"Josh?" he heard himself say, his voice small and scarcely audible, surprising him.

Josh looked up, the old wariness on his face.

Reverend Smith wiped his fingers nervously on a napkin, and looking at his hands, said, "I—I know you and I haven't seen eye-to-eye on things over the years, but I want you to know I appreciate your being here today. I honestly don't know what your mother would've done without you." He paused and looked up. "I don't know what I would've done either."

Josh looked away, shrugged, and wiped his mouth with a napkin. He belched and pushed his plate of chicken bones to the side. "You were right. That was some sho'-'nuf good chicken."

It seemed that he was ignoring what Reverend Smith had said, but Reverend Smith knew better. Josh may have thought he was born with city noise in his blood, but he was acting like a country Negro from the South now as he took a pack of cigarettes from his shirt pocket, took one out, lit it, and tilted his chair back from the table. Reverend Smith continued eating, as if there was nothing else to be said, wondering from which direction and in what way Josh would respond.

"Momma wrote me that the house looks good as new," he said finally. "You tell Carl that he ain't never gon' stay in my house. Nosiree!" Josh laughed loudly. "How is the young Martin Luther King? And how come Momma didn't call him and tell him about Grandmomma?"

"Carl's doing all right, I guess," Reverend Smith responded matter-of-factly.

Josh chuckled. "What do you mean, 'you guess'?"

"He's down in Georgia somewhere with King and the civil rights people." Reverend Smith smiled wryly. "He's about to put me in the poorhouse sending money to bail him out of jail. I'd thought he would've had enough of jail after they made him serve sixty days in the Mississippi State Pen after he went on one of the Freedom Rides."

Josh shook his head in dismay. "I sure would like to see him. I haven't seen him since he was in high school, probably, and that's got to be five or six years ago, at least. But if he don't come to Chicago, ain't no way I'm going to go to Georgia. I always figured he'd be as anxious to get out of the South as I was." Josh chuckled. "When I got off the plane in Little Rock this morning, it was like walking into a nightmare. I hate the South so much that I get depressed if I have to go over to the Southside of Chicago." He sighed. "Well, I know he's going to be upset when he finds out that Grandmomma died, as crazy as he was about her."

Reverend Smith nodded, pushing his plate to the side. "When your mother said she was going to call you, I just assumed she was going to call him, too." An expression of hurt flickered across his face. "I guess I could make excuses for your mother and say that she was too upset to know what she was doing, but, to tell the truth, I suspect that it didn't matter that much to her if Carl came. You were always her favorite, you know."

Reverend Smith could see that Josh did not know how to react to the saying aloud of what they both knew. He smiled uncomfortably. "Guess you say that it's a good thing, since it didn't seem like you were my favorite."

"No, Daddy!" Josh protested, genuinely embarrassed. "I never felt that way."

"Well, you should have," Reverend Smith responded gently. "I've had a lot of years to look back and see my mistakes. You don't have children yet, but if you do, maybe you won't make the mistakes I did."

Josh took a deep drag on his cigarette and stubbed it out among the chicken bones. "Maybe that's why I've never wanted children," he said, not without a trace of bitterness.

Reverend Smith sat quietly for a moment, wounded but not hurt. Hearing what he knew was not revelation.

"You done?" he asked, getting up from the table and holding out his hand for Josh's plate.

Josh got up hastily. "Let me do that, Daddy. Why don't you put another log on that fire while I scrape these plates and do something about all this food."

The rain had stopped and the sudden silence was as startling as it was welcome. Reverend Smith carried wood from the kitchen and piled it in the stove, turning the damper low so the fire would burn for a long while without tending. Joshua cleared the table of the plates and dishes of food, carrying them into the kitchen.

Reverend Smith was surprised and pleased when Joshua returned and sat down again, two bottles of Coke in his hand. He passed one to his father, who thanked him.

Josh lit another cigarette and inhaled deeply. "Momma didn't understand what you were doing out at the cemetery today," he began abruptly. "But, I don't think anything would've satisfied her except Jesus coming down and raising Grandmomma out of that casket." He stared down at his fingers where the smoke curled lazily up from the cigarette. "And when they lowered that casket into all that water, I

almost started screaming and crying my own self. I don't
see how you did what you did today, Daddy. I hate to think
what that scene would've been like if another preacher had
been there."

He looked up at his father, and Reverend Smith met and
held his gaze. Josh looked away after a moment. "If I'd
ever wondered if I could've been a preacher, I know today
that I couldn't have. But I guess I been knowing that since
I was five or six."

"What do you mean?" Reverend Smith asked softly,
amazed by Josh's admission that he'd ever considered the
ministry.

"Well, as you know, I had to go to a lot of funerals when
I was growing up. There's one time in particular though
that I've always wanted to ask you about. You remember
when you had that little church outside Birmingham and
Brother Wilson died?"

"Brother Wilson?" Reverend Smith repeated.

"I believe that was his name. Short man, had a yellowish
complexion and little bitty eyes. I was little at the time so
I never got the full story, but I never will forget that funeral.
There were people standing in the road in the rain. Negroes
came from Birmingham even. I believe I heard somebody
say some white men killed him."

"Oh, Brother Wilson," Reverend Smith said, his voice
dropping. "I didn't think you'd remember that. You couldn't
have been more than six at the time."

"Well, I remember it because you couldn't have gotten
another nigger inside that church if you'd used a shoehorn.
And people were standing outside in the rain like somebody
was about to give out free bar-b-que. I couldn't understand
how that little man could've been that popular."

"Theo Wilson was his name," Reverend Smith said, more
to himself.

"And I remember you preached a long time that day. I mean, a long time!" Josh laughed.

"Two hours and a half," Reverend Smith said seriously.

"That long?" Josh exclaimed, still chuckling.

Reverend Smith nodded. "Theo Wilson worked down at one of the hotels there in town and because he was kinna unusual-looking, the white women were always after him. I tried to tell him several times to be careful. He might look like he was Chinese or Japanese, but he wasn't. Well, we'll never know the whole truth of the matter, but the way the story came out was that he raped a white woman. I know that wasn't true. More than likely some woman staying at the hotel enticed him up to her room. He went and her husband or boyfriend walked in on them and the woman screamed rape. That kind of thing happened all the time across the South.

"Well, about five o'clock one Saturday morning, someone started pounding on the door. I got up and it was his momma. She belonged to my church and all she said was that Theo was in trouble and could I come. I thought he had got thrown in jail for being drunk or something. That had happened once or twice. I got dressed, got in my car with her, and started downtown to the jail. She told me he wasn't in jail and to drive east on the highway out of town. I must've driven ten miles or so before she told me to make a right turn. I turned onto a dirt road and came around a bend and there he was, hanging from a big oak tree whose branches hung over the road so thickly it was like the entrance to a tunnel. He was hanging right there in the middle of the road, naked, with his privates cut off."

"Oh, my God!"

"Wasn't nobody around, but I could see a lot of car tracks in the field on the other side of the road. I never will forget it. The mist was just rising off the field and the birds had started chirping and it was like there was nothing and nobody in the whole world except me and Sister Wilson, that tree, and Theo, and down on the ground beneath him, a puddle of blood. All the blood in his body had run from where they'd cut off his privates."

Reverend Smith stared at his hands for a moment. "I don't know what I would have done if Sister Wilson had started crying and screaming. She didn't and I'll never know why. That was her only child. But we just sat there in the car for a long while, staring at Theo.

"Finally, she said, 'I reckon we should get the law, Reb'n, but seeing as how it was the high sheriff what come and told me to get you to bring me out here, ain't nothing to tell him, is there?' I allowed as to how that was true. Then she went on. 'I knows it be a lot to ask, Reb'n, but you reckon you could get him down somehow and we take him back to town ourselves?' "

"What did you say, Daddy?" Josh couldn't restrain himself from asking.

"What could I say? I can't think of anything I've ever done in my life that I didn't want to like that. I don't know how I did it, but I managed to get up that oak tree, crawled out on the limb, and cut the rope with my pocketknife. I felt kind of bad that there wasn't anybody to catch his body and it had to fall in the dirt like it was a possum shot off a limb. But I climbed down, picked him up in my arms like I did you when you would fall asleep before bedtime, and put him on the backseat of the car. And I drove slowly back to town to the colored undertaker.

"That was Saturday morning around seven, seven-thirty. I stayed at the undertaker's and helped Sister Wilson make the arrangements and drove her home and came on home myself. About noon, there came another loud knock on the door. It was the high sheriff. He was a big ol' red-neck, stomach hanging over his belt like a pig's belly. He had a big cowboy hat on, wad of chewing tobacco in his cheek, and a billy club in his hand. I knew him, because he was always releasing somebody he'd picked up for nothing into my custody. But that day he looked as mean as any white man I've ever seen. Usually he'd call me 'Reverend,' but the minute I opened the door, he said, 'Nigger, if you don't do what I say, you and a lot of niggers in this town got serious, health-threatening problems. You got a funeral to preach tomorrow.' "

" 'Funeral ain't 'til Tuesday,' I told him.

" 'Is you deef? I said the funeral is tomorrow. It would've been this afternoon but that nigger undertaker claims he can't get the body ready.' "

"Well, I found out later that afternoon that the Negroes in town were pretty upset and had got out their shotguns and rifles and pistols, had bought every shotgun shell and bullet they could find in Birmingham and were ready to send some white people across the River Jordan. The high sheriff knew that the more days before the funeral, the more trouble he might have. And I knew that if I preached the wrong kind of funeral, a lot of folks might get hurt or killed. Best thing that could've happened was that it rained. The rain and my two-and-a-half-hour sermon cooled things off, and nothing happened," he finished, not without pride.

Josh was silent for a long while, staring at the drawn shade on the window opposite the table, smoking a cigarette slowly. From time to time he glanced at his father as if trying to decide whether to say something. He lit another cigarette from the butt end of the one between his fingers, and Reverend Smith noticed a slight tremor in his fingers.

"Can I ask you something that's been on my mind for a long time?" he asked, putting out the butt in a saucer and inhaling deeply on the newly lit cigarette.

Reverend Smith chuckled nervously before Josh's hard stare. "Of course."

"How do you know what you did was for the best that day?" he asked intently, leaning forward.

Reverend Smith frowned in confusion. "What do you mean?"

"Seems to me that it would've been better if the Negroes had gone on and killed a whole bunch of white folks that day," he said firmly, and then chuckled bitterly. "I remember a lot, Daddy. More than you might think I do. I remember how you used to grin and say 'yassuh' and 'naw-suh' to white people. I remember how you used to take your hat off whenever you used to talk to white people, and I asked you once why you did that and you really didn't give me an answer. And I remember most of all that time we went down to Bogalusa, Louisiana, to see Uncle Samuel." He laughed mirthlessly. "Yes, I remember that time. You done probably forgot all about it, but I ain't. Uh-uh."

His anger was palpable now and Reverend Smith sat stiffly in the chair at the head of the table and knew that he needed to wait no longer.

"I was ten," Josh continued, staring at the window shade as if he were addressing it. "Uncle Samuel lived on a dusty street near the railroad tracks and right by the tracks was a little grocery store. I got with some of the other boys in the neighborhood that morning and we searched under people's houses and in the fields for old soda-pop bottles to get enough money to go to the movies that night. Took'em up to the store to get the deposit back. We must've had fifty bottles. Two cents a bottle. That made a dollar. Enough to go to the movies plus buy some candy or something.

"We took'em up to the store and the peckerwood gave us fifty cents for the bottles. The other guys took the money and started on out of the store. I said, 'Hey, wait a minute.

We had a dollar's worth of bottles.' They come telling me that that was all right. Wasn't all right with me and I told the man to give us the other fifty cents." Josh laughed. "That ol' cracker turned red in the face, wanted to know who the hell I thought I was." He laughed louder, warming to the memory. "I asked him who the hell he thought he was, trying to cheat us out of fifty cents. He got so red he started to turn purple. Then he asked me my name, and I stuck my little chest out and told him, 'Joshua Smith, Jr.! And if you don't spell no better than you can count, maybe I better spell it for you.' And I did, too. The other boys dragged me out of the store and down the road. I was hot!

"Well, long about five that afternoon I was playing out back of Uncle Samuel's house and heard you call me. I ran around front to see what you wanted and who should I see standing there but that ol' white man from the store, a piece of grass sticking out of his mouth."

Josh shook his head. "Shows how dumb I was. I thought you'd somehow found out how he cheated me and had made him come to the house to give me the other fifty cents. Talk about dumb! You asked me if I had sassed him. I said, 'No, sir! He didn't pay us what we were due.' You asked me again, and I denied it. And then you started taking off your belt, and I wondered, What the hell is going on here? What did I do wrong?

"By this time it looked like every colored person in Bogalusa was standing in the road to see what was going to happen, and Uncle Samuel was standing there with that silly grin on his face looking scared and Momma was crying and that white man was just chewing on that piece of grass, and you took down my pants, took down my drawers, turned my black ass over your knee, and burned me up. And you didn't give no light licks, either. I cried like a baby.

"And then, if that wasn't enough," he continued, his voice trembling with anger, "you told me to apologize to that peckerwood and after I did that, you reached in your pocket and gave him fifty cents. That was the day I made up my mind about two things: One was to get out of the South the first minute I could and never come back, and two was to be as unlike you as possible. And I'm proud to say that I've succeeded on both counts."

There. It had been said finally. Anguished, Reverend Smith understood too late that it wasn't possible for a father to pass on his life's knowledge as if it were an heirloom that could be held in the hand or admired sitting in a corner. Knowledge was something one had to be willing to earn, like a gleam in the eye, or wearing bib overalls to church. "I remember," he said simply. "After your mother put you to bed that night, I went behind the house and cried."

"You what?" Josh asked.

"I cried, because I knew I'd probably lost you. I wanted to put you to bed that night and explain why I'd done it, but your mother wouldn't let me."

"It's just as well, because I don't think I would've been in a mood to listen."

Reverend Smith nodded. "I know, and I don't blame you. Are you in a mood to listen now?"

To his surprise, Josh nodded, almost eagerly. "Yes, I am, Daddy, 'cause I'd really like to know. I really, really would like to know how you justify doing that to me."

Reverend Smith frowned. To justify would be to make it right and he didn't know that it was. And if it was, should it have been?

"Do you remember my telling you not to go to the movies at white theaters?" he asked, after a long silence.

Josh nodded. "Sure do. I never understood that. It didn't

matter to me if I had to walk down the alley and climb up in the balcony. I just wanted to see the movie. And I remember that you didn't want me to drink water out of the colored water fountains in the stores, or get a hamburger at the colored window at roadside places or ride the buses 'cause I would have to sit in the back." He laughed harshly. "Guess you know I did'em all!"

Reverend Smith nodded, but otherwise ignored the taunt.

"Do you remember me telling you not to go to Charlie Nelson's store?" he continued quietly.

"Was that that ol' cracker's name?" Josh asked. "No, I don't remember that."

Reverend Smith shrugged. "Doesn't matter. You didn't obey me anyway."

Josh shifted uncomfortably in his chair.

Reverend Smith stopped, wondering how to put it into words, but only images came—Tremble, Poppa, Brother Emory, Brother Simpson, Ol' Lady Daniels. "I don't know how to explain it to you," he began finally. "I didn't whip you that day because Charlie Nelson was standing there with his .44 sticking in his belt and telling me that if I didn't whip you he would."

Josh's eyes widened. "Is that what he said?"

Reverend Smith nodded once, as if that didn't matter. "Charlie Nelson didn't know that I had my own blue-steel .44 stuck inside my pants next to my belly."

"You did?" Josh was almost as incredulous as a child.

Reverend Smith gave another nod. "Same one I got in my suitcase now. If Charlie Nelson had laid one hand on you, I would've blown him to kingdom come."

Josh smiled ruefully. "I'm totally confused now. I'd been thinking all these years that you whipped me because he made you do it."

"I can understand how it seemed to you," Reverend

Smith agreed, "and that's been a hurting to me all these years. Let me ask you another question?"

"What's that?"

"Did you ever think about what kind of man Charlie Nelson must've been to cheat you out of a half-dollar, and then want to beat you up, you a ten-year-old boy?"

Josh laughed. "Never crossed my mind. I wanted my fifty cents and I'm getting mad right now thinking about it."

"I know," Reverend Smith said sadly, "and that's why I whipped you that day. I wanted you to be free of white folks. They ain't that important, son."

Josh looked uncomprehendingly at his father. "I don't understand, Daddy. You just told me that you would've killed Charlie Nelson."

"But that would've been for you and me," he responded fiercely, "not because of him. I told you not to drink from the colored fountains, or go up to the colored windows at ice-cream and hot-dog places, and to walk to town rather than ride on the back of the bus because it was your soul I was trying to protect. Didn't have nothing to do with being scared of them. Once you know you got your own soul, saying 'yassuh' to a white man don't harm you." He sighed. "I thought that day that if I humiliated you, you would start obeying me just to keep from being humiliated again. And by and by, maybe, you'd understand." He stopped and when he resumed his voice was heavy with sadness. "I went about it wrong, but I still don't know what the right way was."

The silence returned. Reverend Smith stared down at the worn oilcloth on the table, while Josh stared at his hands in his lap. They were relaxed with each other now, though Reverend Smith could not have said how they had moved beyond a lifetime's anger. Maybe it was the saying of what needed saying, though he didn't think they understood any more about the other, or ever would. Perhaps understanding wasn't so important and all the years wanting Josh to understand what he needed to know had been a cruelty mere acceptance would have averted.

"Maybe you would've come up with a new way to know your soul if I'd stayed out of the way," he offered.

Reverend Smith was taken aback when Josh shook his head vigorously and looked at him with tear-glazed eyes.

"But don't you see, Daddy?" he said, his voice breaking. "Don't you see? Carl understands. He's down in Georgia demonstrating and going to jail. And you. You sit there and calmly say that white people aren't important. Then, how come I'm the only one who gets the shakes if I even start thinking about the South? How come I'm the only one who doesn't understand?"

And with this son before whom he had always felt helpless to know what to do or how to do, the familiar anguish of frustration and failure returned, but this time the anger was at his own inadequacies and so it did not seek vengeance on Josh. Accepting this anger as his humanity, he sank beneath it and found a flinty layer of helplessness to succor this child—which he was still—who so needed him, even now.

And the silence returned like a sigh.

Reverend Smith heard a rustling sound at the front door and opened his eyes to see the mail being shoved through the slot and onto the floor. A moment later came the thud of her cane from the bedroom and up the hallway.

"You 'sleep?" she asked as she came into the living room and saw him in the chair.

He chuckled. "If I had been, I wouldn't be now."

She smiled, bending over to pick up the mail. "Bills,

bills, bills," she recited, looking at the envelopes. "And you got a letter here from Louis. What do you want for lunch?"

"I just finished breakfast."

"What time do you think it is?"

"Can't be past eleven."

"It's past one, Reverend Smith."

"I guess I must've stayed out in the yard longer than I thought."

"What were you doing out there?"

"Just looking at the house. It's in pretty good shape. You'll need to get a new screen door for the back, though."

"You can call somebody to come do it as well as I can."

"I'm glad I had the new shingles put on the roof two years ago," he went on as if he hadn't heard. "The foundation is in good order, though. Probably have to get somebody to clean the gutters. One of these boys here in the neighborhood might do it."

"You talk like you don't plan on being around much longer."

"Well, I might not be."

"If you're not, I'm going to be mighty angry at you," she said emphatically. Then she chuckled. "I don't know why I get so upset when you talk like that. You remember the first time you came to Momma's for dinner?"

"Of course."

"Do you remember the grace you gave?"

"Probably not."

"You thanked the Lord for the gift of life and then you said, 'Because one of us might not be here next Sunday.' Little did I know that I was going to have to listen to that line for the rest of my life."

"Well, one of these Sundays it's going to be true."

"You reckon?"

He pushed himself out of the chair. "Well, I believe I'll go sit in the study for a while and do some work."

"You sure you don't want me to fix you a sandwich or something?"

"I'm fine, sweet. Just fine."

Night

There wasn't a doctor in the country who would've given such a prescription.

"I want you to smoke a cigar before you go to bed every night," Doctor Carter had told him.

That had been thirty years ago. He was dead now. Looked like a white man and talked like a colored one. Doctor Carter told Reverend Smith once that he got tired of colored acting scared around him because they thought he was white and the whites talking about "niggers" to him. So he practiced talking like a Mississippi sharecropper and after a while, couldn't talk any other way.

He'd been born and raised in Washington, D.C. His family was well-to-do and were at the top of the Washington Negro social elite. Like many light-skinned Negroes, they passed for white when it was to their advantage. Doctor Carter had gone through Harvard and Harvard Medical School passing. "I ain't ashamed, Reb'n. I always knowed I wanted to be a doctor among our people in the South and I wanted to get the best education I could to be the best doctor I could. And let me tell you something! I lived as a white man for eight years and had a chance to study'em up close. The only thing that got me through was knowing that I didn't have to be white *all* my life." He laughed his high-pitched cackle. "Now, Reb'n, I looks at your body, listen to your heartbeat, and look at the results of these tests, and I can tell that you been living under a lot of stress and tension. That's how come you got this here ulcer and that's what the pain in your stomach is. You eating yourself up,

135

Reb'n. Now, I could give you a whole bunch of pills and all like that, but I guarantee you that if you smoke one cigar before you go to bed every night, and stop trying to save the world, that ulcer'll go away. If you don't do it, I guarantee you that you'll be dead in five years."

Reverend Smith exhaled slowly on the cigar. He was in his pajamas and robe and sat on a wooden chair in the darkness of a small room at the rear of the basement. The only light came from a naked bulb at the foot of the stairs. He could look through the doorway and see boxes and piles of junk stacked on shelves and strewn across the floor, dirt covering them like a layer of skin.

She had been after him for years to clean the basement. From where he sat he could see the ten-inch round picture tube of the first television set, the old washing machine with the hand-wringer, issues of *Life* and *Look* magazines going back twenty years stacked high along the walls, Josh's saxophone, Carl's violin, and things he wouldn't recognize any longer to save his life. But he had never been able to throw any of it out, though he knew he should have. How could he? Things were memory, too.

He smoked the cigar slowly, wondering if Doctor Carter had prescribed one cigar a day not because there was anything medicinal in it, but as a way of getting him to sit quietly in a dark place for a half hour or an hour every day. Doctor Carter was the only one who knew the price he had paid, and not because Reverend Smith had ever told him. It was just there in his body.

Folks saw him in the pulpit or in the tent and thought it was something wonderful to preach to five hundred or a thousand people. But they didn't know about the calls late at night from people in trouble. They didn't know about Doris Blake who had lived down the street from them in Bayou Bottom, whose husband beat her almost every Saturday night and around two A.M., there'd be a banging on the door and he'd get up to find Doris crying hysterically and would take her in, always afraid that one Saturday night her husband, Tommy, would put a bullet in him or through a window of the house. One Saturday night he was awakened by loud shrieks and screams and by the time he got to the door, Doris was lying on the porch, the blood trickling out of the stab wound in her side like tears. People didn't know about the times he'd gotten someone out of jail or of what he'd had to do to get them out.

"You know this nigger, Reb?" Sheriff Haley asked him.

It was about six months after the lynching and he'd received a call late on a Friday night to go down to the jail. He looked at the boy in the cell. Reverend Smith didn't know him. He'd seen him on the street, heard people talk about him, and nobody had ever said anything good. He was a dark-skinned boy, with a head shaped like a football. He had droopy eyes that were bloodshot always, because he did nothing but drink and gamble.

"What's he done?" he asked the sheriff, evading the question.

"Done!" the sheriff exclaimed. "Shit, he was born black and ugly. Ain't that enough? Hell, I know there's got to be a passage somewhere in the Bible that says it's a sin to be so damn black and ugly." The sheriff laughed loudly and Reverend Smith forced himself to chuckle. "Damn, Reb. This nigger is blacker than you and I didn't think there was nobody blacker than you." He laughed again.

"You sho' got a sense of humor, Sheriff Haley."

Sheriff Haley laughed again. "Yep, everybody always said I should've gone on stage."

"Well, I hope this boy ain't in serious trouble," Reverend Smith said.

"That's up to you. I'll let him go if you sing me one of

them good ol' nigger spirituals like my black mammy used to sing when I was a little tyke. If you too proud, then I guarantee you his butt will be on the county chain gang by the time the sun come up Monday morning."

Reverend Smith's hands involuntarily clenched into fists. He knew that the sheriff saw the tension and anger in his body, and was enjoying it. Reverend Smith looked at the boy in the cell behind the sheriff's desk. He was about eighteen and the sheriff hadn't lied. He was ugly and lay on the thin cot in the cell staring coldly at Reverend Smith. The boy didn't care what Reverend Smith did, and Reverend Smith knew that it wouldn't matter if he sang or not. That boy was going to end up on the chain gang or dead in the next five years, and maybe both.

"Any song you like especially?"

"I just loves 'Swing Low, Sweet Chariot.' "

Reverend Smith sang it loudly and when he finished, the sheriff's eyes were brimming with tears.

"Goddam, preacher. You can sang! That took me all the way back to when I was a little boy and Mabel would rock me to sleep in the afternoon singing that song." He unlocked the cell. "Get your ass out of here, boy!"

Once outside, the released prisoner looked at Reverend Smith and spat deliberately by his highly polished black patent-leather shoes.

"Shit! You sing for the white man like an ol'-time darky. I guess you want me to thank you. Well, you can wait until watermelon grows in Hell. I'd die before I'd sing darky songs for that peckerwood."

Reverend Smith grabbed the boy by his shirtfront and slammed him against the wall of the jail.

"If you think I did that for you, you a bigger damn fool than I thought you were. You think I give a damn if he put you on the chain gang? Well, I don't and if you thanked me, I wouldn't accept it. Now get the hell out of my sight before I go inside and ask Haley for his billy club so I can use it on your black ass!" He shoved the boy down the street and walked away.

Nobody knew how many times he'd sung for sheriffs in how many southern towns. Nobody knew how many times he'd gone to the superintendent of schools or the Board of Education, his hat in his hand, a grin on his face, and a song on his lips, to persuade them to hire another colored teacher, or put a new roof on the shack that was called a school.

He remembered it all, with bewildering and shocking shame, when the demonstrations began in Nashville the winter of 1960. He saw the pictures on television of the college students marching and singing songs, freedom songs they called them, and sitting in at the lunch counters at Kresge's, Woolworth's, Harvey's, and other stores where colored shopped but weren't allowed to sit and eat a hamburger or drink a cup of coffee. And after sitting in for a couple of hours, occupying all the seats at the counters so that no one could be served, they marched to a colored church, singing freedom songs while whites lined the curbs, cursing and occasionally throwing bottles or rocks, and had a big rally. Reverend Smith saw one student stand up in the pulpit and shout that this was a NEW DAY and they were NEW NEGROES who were going to STAND UP for their rights instead of BOWING and GRINNING and saying YASSUH and NAWSUH, and sitting there in his reclining chair, Reverend Smith wondered if Carl was in the church cheering and applauding the demise of the old Negroes like him who had accepted debasement as if it were a consecration and acquiesced to humiliation as if it were their precious birthright.

"Isn't that that boy Carl brought here for supper last fall?

The one that ate up all the fried chicken?" Carlotta asked from her chair on the other side of the living room.

"I thought he looked familiar," Reverend Smith said, remembering more clearly now the boy with the rimless glasses, scraggly goatee, and eyes reflecting as much intelligence as a dull hatchet.

"That boy ought to be ashamed of himself," Carlotta continued with contempt. "What does he know about what it was like for us down here before he was born? I'd like to see *him* get folks out of jail, find jobs for people, and do all you did for colored when white folks would've as soon as killed you as look at you."

That was true, but instead of anger at how it had been, or pride in all that he had done, memory thrust through images of places and faces like a knife through an abscessed wound, and the pain, for which there had not been time or space then, oozed out. He wished he could be as certain as Carlotta that that boy with the chin whiskers was wrong.

There were pictures on the television now of some fashion show at a white country club.

"It hurts thinking about those days," he confessed softly, watching a skinny white woman with long, stringy hair walking fast across a stage and twirling around in a dress that looked more like a nightgown than something a decent woman would wear to the supermarket.

"Well, you never acted like it," Carlotta said, pride in her voice. "I used to wonder back then how you could get up in the middle of the night and go get somebody out of jail and come back and go to sleep like you'd just gone to the kitchen for a drink of water. Every time you went out at night like that, I couldn't sleep because I was scared of what might happen to you, and when you got back, I couldn't sleep for being scared of what they might've done to you. And you would never say a word about it the next morning."

"Well, I didn't want to worry you."

"Knowing would've been better than wondering all the time."

"Well, maybe I didn't want to think about it myself," he admitted.

"Can't blame you for that," she said with finality. "Can't blame you for that."

Could he be as generous to himself? Would it have been better to have told her about cutting that boy's body down from the tree, or about the time he'd been driving back from preaching in Montgomery and a carload of drunk peckerwoods forced his car to the side of the road and put a gun to his head, pulled the trigger, and laughed when the hammer fell onto the empty cylinder? They'd almost laughed themselves sick at how scared he'd looked. Should he have told her, or did what he had done—come home, kissed her, talked about the church service, and gone to bed, where sleep tucked the pain into the little creases of his soul, hiding it from view until a time such as now when memory ceded a knowledge too impossible to stand before except when he turned and looked backward?

"You think Carl goes along with what that boy was saying?" he asked uneasily.

"Carl's got more sense than that," she said flatly. "You know he's been marching and sitting in, don't you?" Carlotta continued, almost too casually.

"I had a feeling he might be, but I didn't know it for a fact."

"I didn't either until Bertha Turner called me just this morning and said she was in Woolworth's yesterday. Said if she'd had any idea that the students were sitting in she wouldn't have gone near the place, but she said she was looking for some blue thread and noticed a crowd at the lunch counter. She should've known then what was going on, but she said she had her mind on matching the thread with a dress she's making for her grandbaby and went to see what everybody was standing around for, and said the first one she saw was Carl sitting on one of the lunch-counter stools reading a book. She said he was the best-dressed one there, too. I laughed and told her, 'That was Carl, all right!' "

Reverend Smith chuckled uneasily. It seemed like he was the only Negro in Nashville who didn't think that the sit-ins were the greatest thing since Emancipation. But that was all anybody wanted to talk about in the barbershop the other day.

"Reb'n, I tell you the truth! I wish I was thirty years younger so I could go on one of them sit-ins myself. Makes me so proud to see our young people standing up for all of us what wasn't able to stand up for ourselves. When these young folks get through with this white man's South, ain't gon' be the white man's South no more."

Was he too old to exult that change was coming finally? Or was he merely jealous that he was too old to make history?

All of that was probably true, but not enough so for his soul's assent. Sitting there in his reclining chair and staring at the television where that boy's image had been only moments before, Reverend Smith thought about all he had endured, all he had done, and because it was a NEW DAY, his life had become memories for which no one would have any use as they sat in integrated schools, on buses and lunch-counter stools beside white people. And his pain as he sat there was not only the affliction of memory restored but the lacerating knowledge that his life in slavery's cold shadows was being ground to dust beneath the hard soles of marching demonstrators. A new song was being sung and its melody was freedom. Was he the only one who would remember the simple melody of survival?

Carlotta laughed suddenly.

"What's funny?" Reverend Smith asked, glad for something to interrupt his thoughts.

"Oh, I was just thinking about Carl sitting in at the lunch counter dressed like he was going to have lunch with the Queen of England. I told Bertha, said, 'Girl, if these white folks had any sense, they'd serve him. He'd rather die than drink a cup of Woolworth's coffee.' " She laughed again. "You know what he said to me the other morning?"

"What was that?"

"Said he knew the address of a store in New York where I could send for Hawaiian coffee, and would I do it."

"What did you tell him?" he asked, chuckling in anticipation of Carlotta's reply.

"Told him that if Folger's instant wasn't good enough, he could move to Hawaii and drink Hawaiian coffee to his heart's content. He also told me that there is a new cleaner's downtown that uses French dry-cleaning techniques and that was where he wanted me to take his suits from now on. I told him that he'd better go get his mirror examined if it was telling him that he was French."

She laughed again, then turned to look at Reverend Smith. "You think he'll be all right demonstrating and sitting in?" she wanted to know, the fear apparent in her voice.

"Well, we know this much about him. If one of those peckerwoods puts a finger on one of his suits, Carl will forget all about being nonviolent."

They laughed. "Then we don't have a thing to worry about," Carlotta concluded.

Maybe she didn't, but he did and that Sunday as they sat at the dining-room table eating dinner after church, he told his younger son about those days when death was like a flood whose waters never receded, those times of darkness on sunny days and buttermilk-moon nights, those times when hope was not yet a word and no one cried because the pain was too great to be felt and still live.

"You're lucky," he told him. "You're nine years younger than Josh and about the time you were born was when I decided to give up trying to make a go of it at country churches and became a traveling evangelist. So you grew up in a nice stone house on a shady street in a big city. If you and your brother would ever talk to each other, he'd tell you what the South was like back then. I hope you understand that my generation had it tougher than you do now. We didn't fail and we weren't a bunch of Uncle Toms like your friend said on television the other night."

Reverend Smith stopped himself abruptly, knowing that he had said it all wrong, with too much anger in his voice, too much earnestness in his face, and too much need to have his life remembered as he wanted it to be.

But Carl was looking at him with an understanding smile. "I knew all that, Daddy," he said quietly, "and I'm just sorry you feel like you have to justify your life to me. Do you think I could do what I'm doing if you hadn't done what you did?"

"What about what I heard your friend say on television?" Reverend Smith blurted.

"I told him not to talk about my daddy like that again, that he didn't know what he was talking about."

Reverend Smith didn't doubt Carl, but he didn't know how to believe him, either. He wanted Carl to keep talking, to convince him. And what kind of father needed his son to tell him that his life had been worthy?

He canceled all his revivals that winter to be at home with Carlotta after Carl and a lot of the students were arrested at the end of February. The arrests only increased the size of the demonstrations, however, and more and more whites began coming to town to attack and beat the demonstrators. And on the TV news every night, he saw

Carl, more and more, standing in the pulpit of the church at rallies:

"We are going to bring the city of Nashville to a halt before we will allow it to commit the sin of segregation anymore! And if we must die to stop this evil, we will die!"

The day that Carl's name and their address was printed in the paper, Reverend Smith rummaged through the closet until he found his old blue-steel .44 and sat up at night with the lights off in the house until he heard Carl's car pull into the driveway.

In April, when Carl told him that they were calling a moratorium on demonstrations to negotiate with the mayor and business leaders on desegregating the lunch counters, Reverend Smith was relieved.

"I'm proud of you," he told Carl one evening as the two sat watching television.

Carl looked at him, surprised. "For what?" he wanted to know.

"Well, I like what you say better than that friend of yours."

Carl chuckled. "Roy thinks the problem is white folks. But he's from Detroit. He doesn't understand."

Reverend Smith laughed appreciatively. "How're the negotiations going?"

Carl shrugged. "I never wanted to negotiate. Roy and some of the other kids from the North are the ones who like to sit in a big room and talk to white people."

Reverend Smith was frightened by the lack of emotion in his voice. "Well, I think negotiating is the right thing to do."

"I agree, but you negotiate from strength. When we called the moratorium, we lost our strength. The demonstrations were beginning to hit the store owners in their cash registers and that's what they understand."

What he said made sense, but negotiations were safer.

No illiterate cracker would try to knock his son's brains out with a tire iron in a meeting room. No one would be putting out cigarettes on his neck, or pouring water over his head, and the police wouldn't be dragging him by his feet across the pavement and throwing him into a paddy wagon. And as long as they were negotiating, he wouldn't have to be afraid of somebody throwing a stick of dynamite through the front window.

Two weeks later, when Carl told him that he had convinced the student negotiation committee to call off the moratorium and resume demonstrations that Saturday, Reverend Smith was angry.

"You've got to give it time," he argued.

"Daddy, school will be out in three weeks and everybody will be going back to Detroit, Chicago, New York, and everyplace else. And that's what the mayor knows."

"What did the mayor say when you told him you were going to start marching and sitting-in again?" Reverend Smith asked, ignoring Carl's irrefutable logic.

Carl smiled. "I didn't tell him. Let the chief of police tell him Saturday morning when we bring downtown Nashville to a total standstill."

Reverend Smith couldn't sleep that night for wondering if he had the right to do it. Probably not, but neither had Tremble. However, you did what you had to do, not because you were convinced of its rightness, but because it needed doing, and, if what needed doing also turned out to be right, you thanked God's goodness and hoped you never had to rely on it so totally again.

Reverend Smith knew that the mayor wasn't stalling; he was only trying to find the way to let integration happen and, at the same time, save face for the white people. Carl was too young to understand how to get what you wanted without making your opponent feel that he was giving something up.

The next morning after he heard Carl's car back out of the driveway, Reverend Smith called the mayor and told him that the students were going to resume sitting-in Saturday.

Reverend Smith was waiting in the living room when Carl came in that night. He knew what had happened, because it had been on the news that the students had secretly broken off negotiations and planned to resume demonstrations, but the mayor, in an all-day meeting with student leaders, had convinced them to return to the negotiation table. Reverend Smith had been startled to hear the newscaster add that "Student leader Carl Smith, the son of Nashville's Singing Evangelist, the Reverend Joshua Smith, resigned from the student negotiating committee."

When Carl came in his face was like a carved mask, and before Reverend Smith could explain, he was out of the room.

A week later Reverend Smith was awakened at five A.M. by the house trembling around him as an explosion ripped the spring morning stillness, shattering glass and disintegrating the massive stones of the old house.

He lay still for a moment, unsure if he was alive or not.

"Reverend Smith?" came Carlotta's tremulous voice.

He reached beneath the covers for her hand and squeezed it tightly. From the front of the house came random noises of objects falling as if in delayed reaction, and then there was an eerie silence into which came the creaking sound of a shattered beam or broken window sash swinging back and forth. He was afraid to get out of bed as the acrid odor of dynamite came into the back bedroom on the sudden rush of cool air pouring through the house, or what remained of it.

"Daddy? Momma?" came Carl's tense voice from the hallway.

"Carl?" his mother answered, sitting up in bed. "Carl?"

"Momma? You okay? Daddy?"

"We're okay," Reverend Smith called back. "You?"

"I'm okay."

But they weren't, at least not Reverend Smith and Carlotta. And they wouldn't be. Not wholly. Not ever again. Twenty years later Carlotta was still taking mild sedatives before she went to bed at night, and he slept, but had never been able to sink to the bottom of the well of sleep since.

They dressed quickly and went tentatively into the dining room and stared, tears in their eyes, across what had once been a living room and front porch, to the house across the street, behind which the sun was suffusing the sky with tendrils of light.

"It's your fault!" Carlotta screamed at Carl. "I knew you shouldn't been out there demonstrating and carrying on and getting yourself on TV. You almost got us killed."

Reverend Smith saw Carl look at him, his eyes hard and still. "It wasn't Carl's fault," Reverend Smith said. "If you've got to blame somebody, blame me."

Carl's face did not relax.

"No, Daddy," he said finally. "You didn't throw the bomb, did you?"

And Reverend Smith understood that Carl's anger was not directed at him.

"Daddy, we're going to hit the streets today." Then he smiled. "Whoever threw that bomb just brought integration to Nashville."

Ten thousand Negroes marched to the mayor's office that morning, and they didn't sing songs but marched in a deathly silence, the sound of twenty thousand feet a song of its own. Reverend Smith watched the march on the news that evening at Ralph's and there was Carl at the head of it, the anger an almost indelible part of his features.

When Ralph chuckled and said, "You sho' must be proud

of that boy, Reverend Smith," he found that he was—but yet sad, because there was no anger in him. And there should have been. There should have been.

Reverend Smith got up slowly, his fingers fumbling along the wall before finding the light switch and turning it on. It was a small narrow room he had built for Carl when he was fourteen. Along one wall were bookshelves and a desk. The shelves still held the books of Carl's youth—novels, magazines, and biographies. A long table extended along the opposite wall, and above it were charcoal drawings and watercolor paintings. That was why he had built the room, he remembered now. It was a place for Carl to come and paint, which he said was hard to do in his bedroom.

He stared at the drawings and paintings pinned to the wall with tacks. The paintings were of scenes in the neighborhood—the big elm tree in the front yard, the house, Ralph's house—but the drawings stirred something in Reverend Smith. There was one of a skull and a candlestick and several of naked trees unlike any trees he'd ever seen. It was as if they were skulls, too. But his eyes could not leave a pencil portrait of Ol' Lady Daniels. He knew better, but he was convinced that if he held out his fingers he would touch skin and not paper.

"I guess you probably don't draw anymore," Reverend Smith said to him once.

Carl shook his head. "No, I don't."

He sat on the couch in the living room, legs crossed, looking at Reverend Smith with his customary remote calmness. He had on a light gray suit, pale orange shirt, deep orange silk tie, and highly polished black shoes. But Reverend Smith's eyes kept returning to the manicured nails and the dull gleam of clear nail polish on them, and the unblemished, smooth skin that seemed as if it had never been nicked by a razor, not even the first time he shaved.

"Why not? You were pretty good. Or at least that's the way it looked to my eyes."

Carl shrugged. "Maybe if the sit-ins and all that hadn't started, I might've tried to find out how good I was."

Reverend Smith couldn't remember when they'd had that conversation. It seemed that Carl showed up unannounced at the house every three or four months during the years he was in the civil rights movement. He never gave a reason for his appearances, as if one were needed. He would stay three or four days, and spend most of that eating and sleeping. He never said anything about what he was doing with King, or about what it was like being in jail or getting beat up by some cracker with a baseball bat, and Reverend Smith never asked.

Had he been afraid to know, or was it that being a father was letting your son have his life, even if it meant not being a part of that life?

There was that morning he and Carlotta had just sat down to breakfast and they heard a key open the front door. It was a couple of days after King's funeral and Carl walked in as casually as if he'd just come back from the store. He put his suitcase by the television set in the living room and came into the breakfast room, where he shook his father's hand and kissed his mother lightly on the cheek. Then he went into the middle bedroom, which had been his and was now Reverend Smith's study, took the cushions off the couch, let out the bed, and went to sleep.

That evening they were watching the news on television and the newscaster said that the search for Dr. King's killer was being widened to the entire United States.

"I was there," Carl said quietly.

"Boy, no!" Carlotta exclaimed.

"I was coming up the steps to the second floor of the motel when the shot was fired," he continued tonelessly.

And that was all he ever said about it.

Reverend Smith's vision returned to the portrait of Ol' Lady Daniels and after staring at it for a moment, he turned off the light and sat down again. He dropped the stub of cigar into the coffee can half filled with water beside the chair, and took another one from the pocket of his bathrobe. Slipping the cellophane paper from the cigar and letting it drop to the floor, he lit it, puffing slowly until the fat end glowed in the dark.

How was he supposed to know what a father said to a son? Sitting in the darkness now, he knew he had been foolish not to ask all the questions he had wanted to. What was King really like and what was it like to have been there when he was shot? He knew that Carl would've told him and it occurred to him now, when time was no more and would not be ever again that perhaps Carl had been waiting to be asked, and not being asked, thought his father had not wanted to know.

He remembered sitting on an airplane and having nothing better to do, looked through a magazine a stewardess had given him, and there, staring at him from the page was Carl, a stream of blood like unruly strands of hair coming down the side of his face. Reverend Smith had bought the magazine later and torn the picture out, but never showed it to Carlotta or Carl. He'd carried it in his billfold, not ever looking at it again.

He supposed that if he had ever known what to say he would've shown it to Carl, but he never had. How was he supposed to know what a father said to a son, and especially a son who having just been clubbed by a policeman, stared into a camera lens as if his bleeding skull was a banner proclaiming victory? Wouldn't he have looked foolish to have shown Carl the picture and asked, "Didn't it hurt?"

Josh had seen the picture, too, and joked about it.

"Bet you that cop was left with a handful of splinters, 'cause I know he broke his stick on Carl's hard head," he said, laughing loudly.

Reverend Smith had laughed, too, feeling his laughter a betrayal of Carl. But the deeper betrayal was how much more comfortable he had been with Josh. Every summer since Ol' Lady Daniels's death, he and Carlotta had gone to Chicago and stayed with Josh for two or three weeks. He and Josh stayed up late watching television and went to ball games at Wrigley Field and Comiskey Park.

He had enjoyed the modest success of one son, a postman, who lived only to have a good time, and had been afraid of the son who had given him grandchildren, was a legislative assistant to a congressman, and was trying to make the world a better place.

Yet, Josh never called or wrote and if Reverend Smith had not gone to see him every summer, he would not have seen him at all, while Carl called weekly, and brought his wife and children to visit every Christmas.

Two summers ago he had visited Carl for the first time. He had had no alternative. Carlotta had visited him many times, when Reverend Smith was off somewhere conducting a revival for a month or so. Other times when she visited Carl, Reverend Smith had always found an excuse not to go. But late that spring when Carl called and said, "I want you to see where I live before it's too late," there were no more excuses.

It was the longest five days he had ever lived. Even though Carl took them to see the Kennedy Center and the Capitol and even took them on a special tour of the White House, Reverend Smith went to sleep each night counting the days until he stepped on the plane back to Nashville.

It wasn't only the son who moved in the world with an

ease Reverend Smith had thought was reserved for white people. It wasn't only the apartment with its paintings on the walls and sculptured pieces sitting in niches illuminated by indirect lighting, or the meals where they ate off china so thin he was afraid to press too hard when he cut his meat. He kept telling himself that he was proud to have a son who could've introduced him to the president. He could've enjoyed all this if not for Afton, and hadn't that always been the problem, even before there had been an Afton?

Even the name was foreign to his thick, black lips. It was a name for a woman of the imagination, not a slender blond with green eyes, straight white teeth, and skin that glistened like pearls. He liked her, had liked her from the first time Carl brought her to Nashville after they were married thirteen years ago. She was friendly and knew how to make him laugh. But she was white.

It didn't make sense. Carlotta had looked almost that white the first time he'd seen her. But she was the known in an unfamiliar guise.

Sitting in that living room every night after supper, he knew time had stopped far longer ago than he could've imagined, had stopped maybe before he had been able to count it, because as much as he tried not to, as much as he wanted not to, he lowered his eyes whenever she raised her blond head and looked at him. The lessons of his youth were the humiliation of his old age: He could not look a white woman, his son's wife, in the eye.

She came into the apartment that first afternoon, her long blond hair streaming down her back like combed sunlight, and hurried across to hug them as warmly as she would have greeted her own parents.

"I'm so glad you're here," she said brightly, before sitting on the arm of the chair in which Carl sat.

"It's nice to be here," Reverend Smith said dutifully.

He stared at her, her breasts firm and round beneath a yellow blouse, her long legs extending from beneath the brown suede skirt and crossed neatly at the ankles, and he hated her for having the unquestioning confidence only a white woman could have. That was what separated her from Carlotta, who had only looked white but could never be in the world with the certainty that it was hers. He wanted to kill someone.

He'd stayed up every night the first two weeks they moved into the gray fieldstone house, sat in a chair by the front door, the blue-steel .44 in his hand, listening for the sound of a car slowing down or stopping in front of the house, listening for footsteps on the gravel driveway. No one came. No one seemed to care about the black man, his wife, and sons who had bought the house in the middle of the block. They cared only enough to put up their houses for sale.

During the year before the neighborhood changed, he found his neighbors friendly—the retired couple across the street who were moving to their daughter's in Biloxi, Mississippi, because it was warmer, they said; the young schoolteacher in the house Ralph bought, who said seven rooms were not enough for him and his young bride. They would wave to him as he drove down the street in the black Cadillac he'd bought just before moving into the house and he'd wave back, thinking that maybe the South was changing.

One evening he and Carlotta were sitting on the porch and the schoolteacher from next door and a white man who lived on the corner, bald-headed fellow with eyes like a pig's, and the old man from across the street came over.

"That sure is a nice-looking car you got, Reverend."

He thanked the schoolteacher.

"Too nice for a nigger," said the pig-eyed man.

"Now, you promised you were going to say 'nigra,' Everett," the old man admonished him.

They spoke softly, even politely.

"What Everett's trying to say, Reverend, is this," the old man continued. His long thin fingers were trembling. "When we heard a colored family was moving on the block, we was upset, naturally, you know, but after you moved in and we seen that you're decent, respectable people, everything was all right. But some of the people on the block feel kinna funny that you can afford to drive a big Cadillac while they're driving Fords and Buicks and Chevys. You know what I mean? They feel like it ain't right that a colored man should have the most expensive car in the neighborhood. You understand what I'm saying, don't you, Reverend?"

"It sure would be awful if something happened to that pretty car," the pig-eyed man added, staring directly at Reverend Smith. "And I know the insurance wouldn't pay you what you could get in trade for it."

Reverend Smith was grateful for the feel of Carlotta's hand as it slipped into his and squeezed it tightly.

"You like fish, Reverend?" asked the pig-eyed man.

Reverend Smith managed a nod.

"Well, you just sit right here. I caught a mess of catfish today and I'll go up to the house right now and bring you a couple."

"Don't trouble yourself," Reverend Smith said firmly.

"No trouble at all, Reverend. No trouble at all. Always happy to share with a neighbor."

He sold the car but didn't eat the fish.

That was when he built the room for Carl, he remembered now, and opened the charge account at the bookstore for him and done everything he could think of so that Carl would stay in the house instead of in the yard where he would be seen, where he might be seen by the white girl who lived across the street next door to the retired couple.

He'd seen her shortly after they moved in, sitting on her front porch, her straw-colored blond hair hanging as limp as snails to her shoulders. She had on tight shorts and a brief top and looked to be Carl's age, fourteen or fifteen.

It was a Saturday afternoon. He had taken his wife grocery shopping and Carl was usually at the back door to help carry in the sacks, but even after Reverend Smith honked the horn, he didn't appear. As Reverend Smith put down a sack of groceries on the kitchen counter, he noticed the door to the basement slightly ajar. He went down the stairs and, as he reached the bottom, looked directly into Carl's room and there she was sitting on a chair while Carl sat in front of her, a sketch pad held at an angle on his lap.

"How're you today, Reverend Smith?" the girl called out brightly, her thin nasal accent grating on his ear.

"Just fine. How're you?"

"I'm doing right good, sir."

"This is Ellen, Daddy," Carl turned and said calmly.

"Do your folks know where you are?" Reverend Smith asked.

Ellen giggled. "Gosh, no. I mean, no, sir. I snuck all the way around the block and come in through the alley. Why, they'd tan my butt good if they knew."

"Well, I think it's time you went home before they begin to worry."

"Aw, they went out to East Nashville to see Aunt Viola and won't be back for a long while yet."

"I still think it's time you went home."

"Yes, sir," she responded meekly, getting up and pulling at her brief shorts in a futile gesture of modesty. "Can I see what you drew so far, Carl?" she asked eagerly, coming to stand behind him. "That looks just like me, except it's prettier. Can I have it?"

"It's not finished yet."

"Looks good to me."

"It'll look even better when it's finished."

"Well, I'll see if I can sneak over tomorrow. My folks always takes a nap on Sunday afternoon."

"I'll be looking for you," Carl said. "Let me show you out and introduce you to my mother."

Reverend Smith moved to one side as his son followed the girl up the stairs. He didn't move as he listened to Carl introduce the girl to Carlotta. He heard the two pairs of footsteps leave the kitchen and listened to the sound of their voices—hers high, his low—at the back door. Then the door closed, and as if released, he hurried up the stairs.

"I thought you had better sense than that, boy."

"Don't worry," Carl said evenly. "I got more sense than you think I do."

"Don't look like it to me."

"Why do you think the door to the basement was cracked open? Why do you think the door to my studio was all the way open? If I'd left it to her, they would've both been closed."

Reverend Smith had to admit that he hadn't noticed. "Be that as it may, if she goes home and tells her folks you did something to her, who do you think a judge will believe? You or her? Or what if that pig-eyed man who lives on the corner catches on that she sneaks over here? He's the kind of peckerwood that would kill you in a minute."

Carl nodded. "I thought about all of that. I guess I'll just have to take my chances."

"Take your chances!" Reverend Smith exploded.

"Reverend Smith?" Carlotta interrupted quietly.

"What?" he snapped.

"Why don't you let Carl get the rest of the groceries out of the car? I'm afraid the butter and ice cream will melt and the milk turn sour in this heat."

He waved his arm at Carl in angry dismissal.

"If you tell him the girl can't come over, he might start sneaking off with her. And if the two of them sneak off together, something might happen sure enough."

Reverend Smith thought for a moment. She was right. Was she so understanding because of her white skin? Did she hope Carl would marry the girl, or somebody white like her?

"Things are changing," Carlotta continued. "It's not like when you and I were coming up. And if the adults would just stay out of things, the children would work it out in no time at all."

"But the adults won't stay out, and I'm just afraid what could happen to him."

"I am, too. Frankly, I think he's scared."

"He don't act it."

"I can tell. Maybe if we told him it was all right for the girl to come over as long as one of us was in the house, that would take care of it. I got a feeling that she won't be too interested in coming over if she knows one of us is going to be here."

He nodded. "Well, I guess if my choice is having him or all of us get killed, I don't have much choice."

They were wrong about Ellen. Within a week, she was going in and out of the house like she lived there. Her parents came over several times to get her—a short, fat couple, who looked like twins, their faces flushing red as they stood on the front porch refusing Reverend Smith's invitation to come in and have a cold glass of iced tea, which he'd known they wouldn't. But when Ellen came to the door and told them she'd be home "tereckly," there was nothing her rotund parents could do except grin weakly.

"I hear tell you a preacher. That true?" her father wanted to know.

Reverend Smith exuded ecclesiastical dignity. "You heard correct."

"Well, I reckon she be all right in the house of a man of the cloth."

"You needn't worry. If I'm not here, my wife is here."

They both seemed to relax. "Well, I reckon that's all right, then. Now, if she gets on your nerves too much, you just send her on across the street."

She got on his nerves, but not for anything she did. She was a pleasant girl to have around, though she did chatter all the time. But she helped with the dishes, and after a while, it seemed that she came less to see Carl than Carlotta.

But she was white. Carlotta didn't seem to notice, or care. Yet, when her family moved in late autumn, he was surprised by a heavy sadness.

"I want to thank you, Daddy."

Reverend Smith was sitting on the terrace of the apartment late that last evening, smoking his cigar. Carl stood at the railing, his back to the river and the lights on the other side.

"Thank me for what?" he asked, embarrassed.

"Oh, I don't know. For being you. For having given me so much."

Reverend Smith blew the cigar smoke out in a long thin stream, not knowing how to react to hearing what he had wanted to hear for so long.

"You remember the time we went down to Ouichitta for Uncle Samuel's funeral?" Carl continued, as if there was no need for Reverend Smith to respond. "And you told me

about Brother Emory, and great-great-grandfather, and just
so many things?"

Reverend Smith nodded. "I didn't know you remembered that time."

"Remember it like it was yesterday," Carl said emphatically. "I know it hasn't been easy for you here this week,"
he continued, his voice tentative now. "But I just want you
to know that it means a lot to me that you came. I wanted
you to see where I live, even if you might not understand
it."

"No, I don't," Reverend Smith said with more emphasis
than he'd intended. "I know it's none of my business, but
you make too much money for what you do to be legal, it
seems to me."

Carl laughed. "Don't worry, Daddy. Afton does quite
well at the law firm where she works. I do all right on the
Hill, and, to tell the truth, we could live just on the interest
from Afton's trust fund. And we've invested well over the
years."

Reverend Smith nodded, though the words *trust* and *invested* were foreign to him.

"I know you probably can't see it in my life-style, but I
haven't forgotten all you gave me. You recognize this?" He
reached in his pocket and showed his father a round, gold-
plated watch.

Reverend Smith looked at it. "Can't say as I do."

Carl chuckled. "You don't remember one of those times
I came to Nashville and was rummaging around in the
basement and found this?"

"Is that that old watch?" Reverend Smith asked, surprised.

"Same watch."

"That was my poppa's watch and then mine. I'd forgotten all about that thing. Does it run?"

"I had it fixed. It runs like new, and it's mine now."

They were silent for a long time. Finally, Reverend Smith looked up. "I suppose I shouldn't say this, but if I don't say it now, I might never have the chance again."

"Then, please say it."

"I wish you'd married a colored girl."

Carl was silent for so long that Reverend Smith was afraid. But when Carl finally spoke, it was with laughter in his voice.

"But can't you see that that's what you gave me?"

"What're you talking about?"

"I'm talking about you, Daddy!" he laughed warmly. "I'm talking about you!"

The next morning when it was time finally to board the plane, Reverend Smith found himself released, and though he had hugged her every time before on parting, though he had told her how proud he was to have her for a daughter-in-law, that had been the dutiful father speaking. But this Sunday morning when he put his arms around Afton, it was with the timidity of a Mississippi colored boy, and trembling, he held her to him, closely, with all the unspoken sadness of a life encircled by fear.

He dropped the cigar into the coffee can and made his way slowly up the steps. He was quiet now and for the first time that day, there were no images. The house was dark as he came out of the basement, but he did not need a light to make his way through the breakfast room and dining room to the hallway, where the light from their bedroom shone.

She was sitting up in bed, reading a magazine and looked around anxiously as he came, almost stealthily, in.

"What took you so long? I was getting ready to come down to see if anything had happened to you."

"What time is it?"

"It's almost midnight."

"That late? I had no idea."

"Did you fall asleep?"

"No, I don't think so."

"What do you mean? Don't you know?"

"No," he said pleasantly.

"You worry me sometimes."

"You shouldn't worry, sweet. I'm feeling about as good as an old man could feel, I guess."

"You reckon?" she asked, laughing.

"You're going to wear yourself down worrying about me all the time."

"Well, every night now I just worry while you're in the basement. Suppose something happened to you down there. I might fall asleep and not realize until morning that you had gotten sick down there and died, and I was up here asleep and could've saved you."

"Well, why don't I call somebody in the morning and see if they can rig up some kind of alarm system, some bell or something I could ring when I'm down there."

"I'd sure feel a lot better if we had something like that."

"I'll talk to Ralph tomorrow. I'm sure he'll know somebody. Maybe if Josh can come down this summer, he could do it. He knows about electronics and all that."

"You promise me you'll do it?"

"I'll look into it first thing in the morning. It'll give me something to do tomorrow."

He put one hand on the edge of the bed and lowered himself slowly to his knees. Taking the cane by end, he groped beneath the bed until he found the electric razor and pulled it to him. He laid it on the end table next to the bed, then lowered his head in prayer.

He knelt a long time, eyes tightly shut, but no words came. Yet, it was not as if nothing happened, because the darkness from which the words had always come became a space, and silence rushed at him like a soundless wind, and he did not know if he was moving through the blackness of silence, or if it was moving through him.

The darkness grew, though it had not appeared to have a limit. The higher and wider and deeper it became, the more he burrowed into the silence. What words were adequate to offer God from such vast blackness? What claim could he dare make on the Divine? When awake, he did not know if he was asleep, but now, in this realm with the appearance of the kingdom of sleep, he knew he was awake, more awake than he had ever been, and darkness and silence and love rubbed against him like giant cats warming themselves. He wanted to put out his hand to stroke the darkness and he was sure that if he opened his arms he would enfold love which lay, like a pearl, at the nadir of darkness and silence.

It was his now. He knew that as he opened his eyes and saw her sitting up in bed asleep, the magazine folded against her chest, her glasses still on. He wanted to wake and tell her, but when he tried to formulate the words, there were none.

He pushed himself up, using the cane for support, and taking the electric razor from the table, he went into the bathroom and put it in the medicine cabinet. Returning to the bedroom, he got in bed and, turning off the lamp between their beds, was asleep almost immediately.

The fierce light of the sun awoke him as it plunged like a hawk from the nexus of eternity, plunging hooked, beaked, taloned. It was bright orange and he felt its heat in his chest and like a balloon filling with helium, the sun expanded into a searing yellow and the heat in his chest burst, spreading through his body like a nest of dragons. The sun grew until the blackness of the universe was overlaid by a whiteness as pure as snow at the top of an unreachable mountain peak and he feared that if he did not stop gazing into it that he would be blinded and putting up his arm to shield his eyes, he felt himself fall from the bed and onto the floor and he opened his mouth to say? To cry out? To preach? To sing?

But there were not words or sounds for the knowing which was now his.

Evening

Death wasn't nothing but a walk into the Light, he thought again, sitting down at the table in the breakfast room, ashamed now that he had ever been afraid of that walk.

Carlotta put before him a plate with a boiled chicken breast and rice on it.

"They said on the news that it's going to be hot again tomorrow," she said when he completed grace.

"Well, I saw Ralph this morning and he said he'd come over tomorrow to mow the grass. Maybe he can take a look at the air conditioner."

"Don't do that on my account," she responded. "I'd rather sweat than shiver in July."

"Well, I wouldn't mind having it cool at night. Might help you sleep better."

She laughed. "Me and sleep parted company a long time ago."

He wondered if she remembered when her sleepless nights had begun. He supposed she did, though they had never talked about it, just as there was so much they had never talked about.

Maybe they hadn't needed to then. He remembered the evenings when the front and back doors of the house would've been open now to allow whatever breeze was stirring to waft through the house, and they would sit on the front porch in the metal swing and speak with the neighbors taking evening strolls. They hadn't talked on those summer evenings, because it had been enough to sit beside each other bound by all the time which had been theirs.

He couldn't remember when they had stopped sitting on the porch in the evenings, though it was probably after the bombing. The porch swing had been destroyed, of course, and when he suggested buying another one, she had said no, probably. But maybe he had never made the suggestion.

At some time, too, they had stopped opening the doors to invite the evening cool inside, and without noticing it, accepted as normal that they should live inside during the summer, with shades and curtains drawn.

That was what getting old was like. It was a pulling down of the shades against the world, not a giving up as much as a sweet weariness, with which you wanted to be intimate. Yet, there was a sadness to it, which he had recognized in Ol' Lady Daniels the last time they had seen her, when she sat by the wood stove, rocking back and forth, not talking and not answering when spoken to. Had others seen it in him?

"You must've been hungry," she said, laughing with pleasure.

He looked down at his plate, surprised that it was empty except for the bones of the chicken breast. "I guess I was," he smiled.

"It's nice to see you with an appetite for a change. How about a cup of Sanka?"

"Don't mind if I do," he answered, wanting to please her.

She cleared the table and returned a few moments later with two pink mugs of coffee. "You remember when we bought these?"

He looked at the mug as she handed it to him. "I know we've had them for a long time," he said, wanting to remember.

"We used to have four," she hinted.

He smiled. "We bought these right after you came to Atlanta, when I was getting ready to begin seminary."

"Well, I'm surprised you remembered," she said, obviously pleased.

He chuckled. "Now, don't ask me where the house key is."

She laughed with him. "When I was lying back there in the bed this afternoon trying to take a nap, I got to thinking about those days, for some reason." She shook her head. "I still can't believe I did that."

"Did what?" he asked, taking a sip of coffee.

"Rode all the way on the train by myself from Pine Grove to Atlanta. And if I think about it too much, I still get a little mad about you going to Atlanta first and leaving me behind."

He nodded, but had no need to say that he had left her only because she had refused to come with him, claiming that her mother needed her. It wasn't until many years later that Ol' Lady Daniels told him that she had made Carlotta get on the train. "I told her her place was with her husband now, and that I wouldn't be much of a momma if I didn't make her go to you."

Reverend Smith nodded again. "Must've been scary for you," he offered.

"Scary!" she exclaimed. "I'd never been out of Pine Grove in my life. Of course, people now wouldn't understand what was so scary about it. Carl's children flew out to California by themselves this summer to see Afton's people."

"Not back in our time," he commented.

"No, indeed!" she agreed emphatically. "I was so scared I thought I was going to die. And what made it worse was riding in the white coach and passing for white."

"That was the safest way."

"Oh, I know that." She laughed loudly. "I never will forget the look on the conductor's face when he helped me off the train in Atlanta and you walked up and hugged me."

Reverend Smith chuckled. "I'd forgotten all about that. Everybody in the station, white and colored, stopped what they were doing and stared at us. We were lucky that that's all they did."

She nodded. "We were lucky a lot of the time, you know."

He looked at her. "What do you mean?"

"You remember the time we drove down to see Louis in Moss Point, Mississippi, right after he got his first teaching job?"

He smiled, not trying to remember just yet, wanting instead to savour the voluptuousness of shared memory. It was as if there could be no marriage until the act of remembering was all they were capable of, all that they desired, and what was remembered was not as important as remembering-as-an-act-of-being.

"You remember the time I mean?" she asked again.

He nodded. "You mean that time we got stopped by the highway patrol."

She laughed now. " 'Nigger, ain't you got better sense than to drive through Mississippi with a white woman in your car?' " she said, imitating a white southern accent.

Reverend Smith smiled weakly. "I thought I'd had it for sure that time."

"What did you tell him?" Carlotta asked, in eager anticipation of hearing what she already knew.

Reverend Smith's smile broadened. "Well, I know there was no way I could convince him that you weren't white, so I just said the first thing that came into my head. 'She ain't white! She's an Indian squaw, suh!' I put a whole lot of emphasis on that 'suh,' too." He chuckled, warming to the memory. "He looked at me real hard, then stared over at you real hard. 'Nigger, I ain't never seen no Indian that white-looking. We got Indians down here in Mississippi and don't none of'em look like her."

Carlotta was laughing harder.

"I looked at him and said, 'That's because they southern Indians.' I knew I had him then, 'cause he gave me a confused look, so before he could think of anything to say, I just kept talking. 'She's from a tribe what lives up in Montana. You know, boss, it stays so cold up there, being close to Canada and all, and the cold just takes all the color out of the Indians.' My heart was beating so hard I thought it was going to come through my chest, and I said to myself, 'I know he ain't fool enough to believe that,' but all he said was 'I'll be goddammed!' "

Reverend Smith laughed warmly in appreciation of himself. "Do you remember him sticking his head back in the window and asking you to say something in Montana Indian?"

"I'd forgotten all about that!" she exclaimed, laughing so hard her eyes filled with tears.

"I have to give you credit. You didn't even blink an eye."

"I was too scared. I'd had one year of German in high school and I said the first thing I remembered: The pen is on the table. I don't know how it goes now, but I figured he wouldn't know the difference."

"He looked at me and asked what you'd said."

"And you told him, 'She said this is a very pretty state you have here.' "

They laughed again, and when their laughter quieted, Reverend Smith shook his head. "It's hard to believe some white people could be so dumb and ignorant."

"We'd better be glad they were."

He nodded. "That's the truth."

The coffee was cold now, but they sipped as slowly as if vapor were coming off it.

"Josh was about seven then," she added.

"Was he?" Reverend Smith asked, surprised. "I don't remember him being there that time."

"I bet he does," she said flatly.

Reverend Smith didn't doubt that, but Josh would remember only the humiliation and not the victory he and Carlotta had just celebrated. It was not a memory that would have bound son to father.

"You ever think about how much easier your life would've been if you'd married somebody else?" Carlotta asked, almost too casually.

"What're you talking about?"

She didn't answer immediately, but drained her mug of coffee, grimacing at how cold it was. "I was just thinking about how the colored were as bad as the white. They just did it in a different way."

"What're you talking about?" he repeated, more sharply.

She smiled. "I guess I should be mad that you haven't known all these years. I'm not, though. I guess if you had known, it would've made it worse."

"Will you tell me what you're talking about?"

"I'm talking about how the women treated me in every church you ever pastored," she began. Her tone was matter-of-fact and without self-pity. She smiled as she continued. "Or didn't treat me would be a better way to put it. I'd stand around after church waiting for you and nobody would come up and talk to me, but I'd see the women batting their eyes at you, smiling women's smiles at you, knowing I was standing there looking. It seemed like they thought it was my fault that I looked white." She frowned. "They thought that I had had it easier because I looked white, so they wanted to make me pay for it, I guess. It didn't hurt me for myself, but it would hurt me for you when, after two or three years at a church, you would have to move on to another one. If you'd had a wife who looked like what they thought a preacher's wife should've looked like, you would've gotten that big church in Detroit or Chicago you always wanted."

Reverend Smith looked at her, puzzled, as if his aged mind was not able to grasp what she was saying. He hadn't stayed at one church for long because . . . because? At the time he had thought it was his own restlessness and ambition. Going from Macon to Selma had been a step up, but after he told Brother McGhee to kiss his ass he'd known he wouldn't last more than the year of his contract in Selma. From there he'd gone to Bayou Bottom which had been a step down and had lasted only a year. From there he'd gone to Bard, Oklahoma, then Trenton, Arkansas, and Milo, Mississippi, Wausau, Alabama, and every year there were invitations to come for interviews at churches in Memphis, Little Rock, Atlanta, and he'd preach a guest sermon and turn the church on its steeple almost, but some other preacher would be offered the position. Yet, these same churches would invite him to preach if the pastor they'd hired instead of him went on vacation or was away at a conference, and the members would say, "We sho' wish we'd hired you, Reverend Smith," but no one would ever tell him why they hadn't.

"I was so glad when you decided to give up the churches, get a big tent, and take a chance at being a traveling evangelist."

"Well, the Lord works in mysterious ways. Being a traveling evangelist worked out better than any church ever would have. I made more money at it, too."

"Yes, everything worked out all right," she said, pushing

herself out of the chair with an exaggerated groan. "Well, let me get in here and straighten up the kitchen and do the dishes."

He knew he hadn't answered her question, and he wanted to, but when she spoke to him from the heart and revealed her love, it was as if he had been offered a gift he didn't know how to receive. And why was that?

"I'm not sorry I married you," he said hoarsely as she went slowly into the kitchen.

She laughed and he thought he saw her blush. "I know that," she returned. "If I didn't, I wouldn't have asked."

He would've wished for a more gentle response, which was the same as wishing she were another woman. He smiled and reached beneath the chair for his cane.

"What do you think you're doing?" she wanted to know when he came into the kitchen and took a dish towel from the drawer.

"Oh, I feel pretty good tonight. Thought I'd dry the dishes."

She laughed with pleasure. "Well, it'll be nice to have some company." Carlotta sat on a stool at the sink. "Of course, as few dishes as we dirty up nowadays, you won't work up a sweat."

He chuckled. "No, I reckon not."

She rinsed off a plate and handed it to him. "I have some pig feet in the freezer. You think you might want them tomorrow?"

"I'll give'em a try."

"Well, let me get up now and take'em out or I'll forget I ever said anything about it."

"You stay there. I can get them."

"Just put'em on the shelf there in the refrigerator."

He took the package of two small pig feet out of the freezer compartment and put them in the refrigerator. They did the dishes in silence, she handing him the dishes, glasses, and silverware one at a time.

"Well, that's taken care of," she said when they were done. "I appreciate your help, sir," she said with mock formality.

"Madam, you're quite welcome."

"Well, I think I'll go back in the bedroom," she said, moving past him.

Before he could think of what to say to hold her there for a few minutes more, to hold her until he knew the words, or knew that there were none, he heard the cane thudding against the rug as she moved through the dining room and down the hallway to the bedroom and it sounded like a hammer driving nails into a coffin.

He stood by the kitchen sink, his pants hanging as loosely as a dead leaf on his withering frame, an old man whose life had been given to knowing the right words to say to the bereaved, the sick, the troubled, the helpless, and yet, when he wanted words the most, none came. There were only the images which came not smoothly and continuously as on a reel of film, but singly, as if engraved on commemorative postage stamps.

There was the one of him and her standing before the black woodburning stove in the tiny kitchen of their house in Atlanta, and him showing her how to start a fire with the kindling and how to regulate it for even heat, and how to cook. She stood there, tears of frustration and anger on her face, tears of anxiety, also, because living apart much of the first year of the marriage, he assumed she'd done the cooking when he came to see her every weekend, never thinking it was her mother who'd made the rich chicken and dumplings, baked the hams with brown sugar, and fried chicken so crisp and juicy it tasted like a dessert.

There was another image, one that would not have come

if they had not had coffee and talked, or if it had, he would not have bothered to look at it. Now he stared at it and another like it and another as they came in quick succession. They were all the same. Only the interiors of the churches were different. She stood in the church vestibule in a corner near the door watching him, watching the women hugging and kissing him, and then walking past her, and if they spoke, it was a curt "How you this morning?" or simply, "How do?" She stood, waiting, watching, her thin lips betraying no expression.

He saw her now as if for the first time, a young white woman, her long black hair parted in the middle and flowing down her back. She was plain-looking and the very simplicity of the plainness gave her a disturbing beauty. It was as if she had decided at some early age to contain all of who she was inside herself, revealing nothing for others to admire or abuse, and the discipline of her restraint revealed itself in the dark eyes, whose gaze seemed capable of peering into dark glass and finding the reflection. The aura of stillness surrounding her bestowed a quiet dignity and forbidding dignity that seemed impenetrable. Who was he not to have noticed, not to have known, not to have cared that those who greeted him with hugs and kisses passed by her as if she were a plaster statue.

He stood by the sink, the images entering him like the swift, repeated thrusts of a knife.

It was during the Depression. He had a church in a little country town called Stockard, Arkansas. They'd lost all their savings when the bank failed. He took another church in another little country town and traveled back and forth between the two trying to earn enough to make ends meet. The people didn't have any money either, but in the summer they paid him in tomatoes and turnip greens and chickens. In the winter, all the vegetables they canned that fall were about used up and he didn't know what they were going to do. Josh was two or three at the time.

Reverend Smith looked for odd jobs in Stockard and the surrounding towns. He'd done just about everything at one time or another—carpentered, farmed, taught school, barbered, been an undertaker's assistant, painted houses—but with white folks going hungry, who was going to hire a Negro?

One Thursday night he came home, tired and depressed, and she told him she had some good news. He could certainly use some, but when she told him that she had a job cooking and cleaning for a white family, it was one failure too many. He couldn't seem to stay at a church for more than a year; he hadn't even been able to hang on to what little money they'd had, though the bank's failing hadn't been his fault but it was his loss; he couldn't make a living from two ramshackle churches, and now, he couldn't even support his wife and baby and before he knew it, he slapped her hard, once, twice, across the face, knocking her to the floor. No woman in his family had ever worked for white people. Didn't she understand that one of the reasons he was a preacher was so that he wouldn't have to work for some red-necked peckerwood? And didn't she have sense enough to know what happened to colored women who worked in homes where there was a white man? Did she think any white man would keep his hands off her, for there was nothing they liked better than a colored woman who looked white, 'cause they could have what they thought was the best of both worlds that way?

She stared up at him from deep within her dark eyes, the tears standing in them like a tub filled with rainwater, but they did not spill over. Josh ran to her from where he'd been standing in the doorway of the kitchen, yelling and crying, "Momma! Momma!" She took him in her arms, rubbing his back softly until his sobbing quieted, and then, she got up, still holding the baby, and walked into the bedroom.

The next morning at breakfast she said that she'd sent the woman a note by one of the boys in the neighborhood telling her that she wasn't going to take the job, and neither of them ever alluded to that awful evening again.

Does it require a lifetime to know shame? he asked himself, a tear flowing down his cheek. He wiped at his face with a trembling hand. And does it take all of a lifetime to realize that what we know so convincingly as our lives are merely imaginings, poses we strike because we think of everyone around us as cameras whose only functions are to record our images?

He walked slowly from the kitchen and into the bedroom. She was sitting on the edge of her bed in her nightgown, filing her nails with an emery board.

"Did you ever forgive me?" he asked hoarsely.

She looked up at him, her eyes showing bewilderment at first and then the clarity of knowledge. She looked back at her nails, scraping at them less surely now. "I don't know," she said finally, still not looking at him. "I just don't know," she repeated softly, and then lay the emery board on the night table, groaned, and said, "Well, I guess I'd better get on in there and take these teeth out. I went to sleep with them in my mouth the other night." And she laughed.

As she walked past him, the stab of her cane barely missing his foot, she said, "I stayed, didn't I?" She laughed again. "Momma said you did the right thing. I wrote and told her that was the last time I'd ask her opinion about something. What made you think of that after all these years?" she wanted to know, stopping to look at him from the bathroom door.

"What we started talking about at supper brought a lot of things back and I got to wishing I'd done better."

It sounded like a plea for forgiveness, but it was only a confession, which sought no absolution other than what was conferred in the saying and the being heard. So he did not wait for a response, but turned and went wearily up the hallway and into his study where he sat down at his desk.

We don't know who we are, he thought, until we turn and look back at who we were. That's why Death wasn't nothing but a walk into the Light which would take him in and warm him and hide him and let him rest after working in the vineyard of the Lord. There was nothing to fear when you could see all the way back like he could now.

God had always walked with him, like the time in Stockard. She wouldn't speak to him, wouldn't even let him come near Josh to hold him or play with him. He couldn't find a job no matter how much he looked and was beginning to wonder if he was going to have to swallow his pride and ask her to go work in the white folks' kitchen. Then, one morning a white man came to the door.

"Preacher, I'm from the government and the government is going to be giving out relief food to the poor and hungry." He was a little man, with a big floppy straw hat whose brim kept falling over into his eyes. "We need somebody to pass out relief food to the niggers and I hear tell you an honest boy." He took off the straw hat and mopped his bald head with a big white handkerchief. "Gov'ment will pay you five dollars a week and you can take as much food for your family as you need."

It was hard work, because he had to keep accurate records of who got how much for when the little man in the big straw hat came around to see how much food had been distributed.

One morning a Negro came to the back door. He was

drunk, sloppy falling-down drunk. He said he was hungry and his family was hungry and could he please have some food?

Reverend Smith knew that government regulations forbade giving food to anyone who was intoxicated and if he gave the man food and it was found out, he would be out of a job and food.

He looked at the Negro, a tall, lanky young man in bib overalls. His eyes were big and rounded, and bulged from his head like frogs' eyes. His thick lips were parted and his mouth hung open like he was retarded. Reverend Smith knew he was lying and that he would take the flour and lard and dried beans and sell them to the first person he saw for the price of a bottle.

But what if he was telling the truth? Reverend Smith never knew why but he gave the man food and wrote in his records that he'd given it to some strangers driving through town on their way to California. That wasn't unusual. There were always people knocking on his door in the middle of the night who were traveling through and needed a little food to help them on their way.

After the government man checked his records at the end of the week and initialed them, Reverend Smith thought no more about it. A year passed and one Saturday afternoon he needed gas to get to Chockville where he'd taken another church. He was especially eager to go that Saturday because the people were going to pay him cash money on Sunday, but there he was with scarcely enough gas to get out of town and not a penny in his pocket.

He remembered getting up that Saturday morning and kneeling beside the bed and praying for a long time. Then he kissed Carlotta and Josh good-bye, got in his car, and drove to the center of town.

He pulled into a filling station, wondering why he was

doing that, but he stopped at the gas pump as if his pockets were full of money. Back in those days white men wouldn't pump gas for colored. They hired colored for that. He sat in the car next to the pump and looked toward the station where the white owner sat at his desk staring at him. Finally, Reverend Smith saw him turn and yell at somebody, and in a moment, out came a colored man from the garage wiping his hands on a greasy rag.

The man looked at Reverend Smith and started grinning. Reverend Smith wondered what was so funny.

"Reverend Mister Smith," the Negro said.

Reverend Smith smiled politely. "How're you today?"

"I'm fine, suh. Just fine. You wants me to fill it up?"

Reverend Smith laughed nervously. "Well, that's what I want. But I won't be able to pay you until Monday."

The man hadn't stopped grinning. "Aw, I wouldn't take your money no time. No, suh. I fill it up right now."

Reverend Smith was convinced that the man was a mental patient. Or he should've been.

The man filled the car with gas and still grinning, asked, "You remember me?"

Reverend Smith had to admit that he didn't.

"You gave me food one time when me and my family was hungry. I was 'shamed to come to your house that day 'cause I'd been drinking, but you give me food anyway."

Reverend Smith remembered then. "You seem to be doing better now."

"Oh, yes, suh. Now, don't you worry none about paying for this gas. It's all taken care of, and anytime I can do something for you, you just come straight here."

He could recall countless stories like that, so-called co-incidences that were plainly the work of God. It wasn't as easy to see God in the shadows, though.

He hadn't understood how come it seemed like God

wanted to kill him a little at a time. Since he was going to die one day, why didn't God just take him instead of letting him see death coming one step at a time? Like that morning at the beginning of last year when he was driving to church. He passed his exit on the expressway and even now didn't understand why he decided to back up instead of continuing on to the next exit. But he stopped the car, put it in reverse, and started backing up, cars blowing their horns as they swerved around him and him wondering what they were honking at and the next thing he knew there was the sound of a loud crash and he felt himself thrust into the steering wheel and the car spinning onto the shoulder of the road and crashing into the guardrail.

Where had that other car come from? It had been a young white fella and his pregnant wife and their car was lying on its side straddling the highway. After a while the police came and the ambulance came and took the white fella's pregnant wife to the hospital looking like she was dead. He stood alone beside the guardrail and cars passed slowly with people gawking at him as if it were a carnival sideshow. The police asked him a lot of questions, but he couldn't remember what had happened or why he'd been backing up on a busy highway. He didn't believe he'd done it and somehow it must all be the young white fella's fault, because there was a time, like back in 'forty-six when he'd driven all the way from Denver, Colorado, to Sacramento, California, without stopping, not because he'd wanted to but because there was no place in between for colored to stay. And there weren't superhighways back then, either. Just two-lane roads and you couldn't make good time like you could now because the highway went through every little town there was and through the heart of every big city. But he'd done it without even pulling off on the side to take a nap. Now they were trying to tell him that he couldn't drive to church even without almost killing somebody.

He sat in the hospital waiting room all that afternoon. What would he do if the girl and her baby died? When the doctor told him that she and the baby were going to be fine, he cried.

He'd had to pay all the hospital bills plus a couple of thousand dollars so the young white fella wouldn't sue him. His driver's license was taken away for a year and when he went to take the test to get a new one he'd failed. So he had had nothing but time to realize that he didn't want to live if he had to depend on different ministers and neighbors to drive him to church, to take his wife shopping, to bring him cigars from the drugstore. He was ashamed to live if he couldn't do better than he was doing and he knew that he would never do better but only worse and worse. Would he end up in a home like Carlotta's brother, who had to have somebody wipe him when he got off the toilet?

Before that happened, he had to write down the facts at least. Was it that he didn't trust anyone else to write his obituary, or was it only that Carlotta or Carl or Josh would not remember the names of all the churches, the dates and cities of the biggest revivals he'd conducted? Or was it the deeper need to know that he had done something of significance?

He'd been called the "Colored Billy Graham." That was what a white newspaper in Des Moines, Iowa, had written when he'd conducted a month-long revival there. The Negroes had laughed about the article, " 'cause, Reverend Smith, you better than Billy Graham. Of course, it's hard for white folks to conceive that anybody colored could be better than them at something." While the whites may have compared him to Billy Graham, among colored he was known as the "Singing Evangelist." There was a time when he

walked through the colored section of any city in America
and at least one person would stop him and say, "Ain't you
the Singing Evangelist?"

It wasn't a title he'd bestowed on himself, and, to tell
the truth, he'd never thought of himself as much of a singer,
but often, in the middle of a sermon, something would
swell up inside him until the only way to express it all was
to sing. And it was this which grabbed the imagination and
spirits of the people, the way he would have them singing
the old songs, the ones that had been washed in the blood
of slavery.

> *Do Lord, Do Lord,*
> *Do remember me.*
> *Do Lord, Do Lord,*
> *Do remember me.*
> *Do Lord, Do Lord,*
> *Do remember me.*
> *Do remember me.*
>
> *When I am dying*
> *Do remember me.*
> *When I am dying*
> *Do remember me.*
> *When I am dying*
> *Do remember me.*
> *Do remember me.*

He didn't know where the songs came from, because he
could've sworn he'd never heard them until they came from
his throat. Yet, invariably after a service, some old person
came up to him and said, "Reb'n, I ain't heard that song
since I left from down home. My ol' granmamma used to
sing that. I'd lie in bed at night and hear her in the other

part of the house singing that and getting happy just like it was church time Sunday morning. I never thought I'd hear that song again until I met her up in Glory."

Where had he heard it? Or was it that if you were born in a certain time and a certain place, you, too, were washed in the blood of slavery and knew the song if you only opened your mouth and sang.

Known as the Singing Evangelist, he conducted revivals in most of the 48 states, the West Indies, and South America. Among his greatest were Chicago, 1948, Detroit, 1952, New York, 1956, and Atlanta, 1963. That was what was wrong with an obituary; it could be only names and dates, and what were they without memory and memory would die with him. Who would there be at his funeral to remember the people filling all the folding chairs in the big tent, people standing in the vacant lot and spilling over onto the sidewalk and then into the street and the police came to tell him that his revival meeting was disrupting traffic and he'd have to close up. That was what happened in Detroit in 'fifty-two.

"You mean to say you gon' close me down because the people want to hear about Jesus Christ?" Reverend Smith told the white policeman with the gold shield on his hat.

"Now, Preacher, I didn't say that," he said, flustered.

"You don't think that's what you said, but it is. These people not coming out here to see a ball game or a crap game or to fight. They're coming to be saved from sin. You want to stop people from being saved from sin?"

The policeman smiled ruefully, took off his hat, and scratched at his head. "Preacher, if you can talk that persuasively about Jesus, this is going to be the most Christian part of town. Let me call the station and see what I can do about getting a couple of men assigned to traffic control down here."

"God won't forget you."

"If you say so, I don't doubt it."

An obituary couldn't tell about the power that came through him when God was present. He could preach two, three hours a night, seven nights a week for a month without getting hoarse or sick. And unlike a lot of evangelists, he didn't have a band and a big choir behind him. He didn't dress in mink coats and jewelry like Daddy Grace. Other evangelists put on a show because they were afraid the people wouldn't come out otherwise. He depended on God.

Why could an obituary not record memory, too? He was a hollow shell left on a beach by the tide and anyone holding him to their ear would hear only an emptiness echoing in eternity.

Then he remembered sitting at that same desk in the middle of a winter afternoon the year after they had gone to see Carl. Carlotta was napping in the bedroom. He sat, a blank sheet of paper before him, not trying anymore to leave behind what he would have to take with him. He looked around the room, and his eyes stopped at the painting on the wall Carl had done in high school.

It was of an oblong mask with a wide mouth that extended beyond the parameters of the face. Painted in light and dark brown shades, it looked like something out of Africa. He'd always wanted to ask Carl what he was thinking when he'd painted it. It had been twenty years since he'd claimed Carl's room as his study, but he had never been able to take down the painting. He was waiting for those wide lips to speak, certain that they had, that they were, but he couldn't hear the words, or maybe he didn't understand the language.

How could a child paint something that his own father couldn't understand? How could the son be something beyond the father, something other than what the father knew had come from him? Suddenly he was looking down at himself as if through the eyes of God and he saw an old black man sitting at a gray metal office desk. That was all. An old black man. And he thought about Poppa who didn't get to be old, and Samuel who didn't get to be old, and Dallas, who merely aged like a discarded board lying in an empty field.

Carl was still in high school when Samuel's wife called and said that he'd died of a heart attack and she wanted to bury him in the family cemetery. Reverend Smith didn't ask her why, didn't tell her that the old cemetery was probably so overgrown with weeds now that he wouldn't be able to find it, didn't say that Sammy didn't deserve to be buried there. He simply agreed, hung up the phone, and went in the kitchen to tell Carlotta.

"That was Leora. Sammy's dead."

"Reverend Smith, no!"

"Dropped dead from a heart attack."

She shook her head mournfully. "He wasn't as old as you."

"Six years younger. Just turned fifty a couple of months back."

"Well, I guess I'd better start packing," Carlotta said, wiping her hands on a dish towel.

"What time does Carl get in from school?"

"Three."

"Well, go ahead and pack for all of us. I'll call the school and we can pick him up and go on and get on the highway."

"You're not thinking about driving all the way to Ouichitta tonight, are you?"

"No. I'll call Louis. We can stay overnight with him in Memphis and all drive down to Ouichitta tomorrow."

He had never reconciled himself to Sammy's death, so abrupt that it seemed like a rebuke from God. What would

Tremble have thought about one of his descendants ending up as a sharecropper on the same plantation he'd risked everything to be free of?

The next morning when they crossed into Mississippi on Highway 61, he remembered a verse he'd overheard the blues singers on the Wellington plantation sing:

> *Lawd, that 61 Highway*
> *Is the longest road I know.*
> *Lawd, that 61 Highway*
> *Is the longest road I know.*
> *Runs down from Chicago*
> *To the Gulf of Mexico.*

He didn't know if that was true. He'd promised himself that he would find out one day, but he'd forgotten and now it didn't matter.

It was a straight, narrow two-lane highway that certainly seemed as if it had no end. His was the only car in either direction, and except for an occasional shack in the distance, Reverend Smith and those in the car could've been the only people alive.

"When's the last time you were down this way, Joshua?" Louis asked from the backseat where he sat with Carl.

Reverend Smith thought for a moment. "I can't remember. It's been a while, though. I can tell you that."

"You ever been down to the homeplace?" Louis asked Carl.

"No, sir. This is my first time."

"I thought you'd been down here," Reverend Smith said to Carl.

"Not that I remember."

"Don't feel bad, Joshua," Louis put in. "I live an hour away, and I don't suppose I been down here in ten years.

I think the last time I came was when Sammy moved on to the Wellington plantation. It hurt my heart so much to see my own brother living like a common sharecropper, that I just never came back."

Louis was the shortest and youngest of the brothers. His smallness was emphasized by his girth, which gave him the distinct appearance of a solid roundness. He always wore a three-piece suit, and the vest completed the picture of health and prosperity he projected.

"Maybe that's why I never came. I guess the last time I saw Sammy was when he was living down in Jackson? Is that right, sweet?"

Carlotta thought for a moment. "I believe so. He was trying to make a go of it as a mechanic. That was Jackson, wasn't it?"

"That's right!" Louis put in. "Had a little hole-in-the-wall place off Lynch Street."

Reverend Smith nodded. "I asked him then to let me loan him the money to send him to automotive school so he could get top-drawer training. Leora begged him, too."

"That was right after Daniel was born," Carlotta added. "I remember, because she was having trouble nursing at the time."

Louis grunted. "I believe Sammy probably failed at more jobs than most people ever have. Mechanic, barber, roust-about."

"He was a redcap for a while at the station in Memphis, wasn't he?"

"That's right!" Louis said. "A few years before I moved there."

"And he worked at the lumberyard in Bogalusa," Carlotta remembered.

"I didn't know about that one," Louis said.

"Didn't last long," Carlotta said, laughing. "Of course,

he wasn't able to stay there after Josh almost got us all lynched."

"What did Josh did, Momma?" Carl asked eagerly from the backseat.

"Nothing you need to know about," Carlotta said firmly.

"Aw, Momma. Come on. I know Josh was always causing trouble."

"And if you don't be quiet, I'm going to cause you some trouble."

"Yes ma'am," Carl muttered, retreating quickly.

They were silent for a moment.

"Why couldn't he ever find himself, Joshua?" Louis asked, anguish in his voice.

That was the question Reverend Smith had been trying to answer for himself since Leora's call.

"It always seemed to me," Carlotta said, "that he got caught between Dallas and Reverend Smith."

"How so?" Reverend Smith wanted to know.

"Oh, I don't know. It was just one of those things. I remember when we were living in Atlanta and you came back here to get Louis to come live with us and how bad you felt that you hadn't been able to convince Sammy to come, to get him away from Dallas's influence."

"I remember that!" Louis affirmed. "I remember thinking at the time that it was like me and Sammy were raised by two different daddies. Dallas was his and you were mine."

Reverend Smith still didn't say anything, as he kept the car at a steady sixty miles an hour. Sammy had been the best-looking of the three brothers. Walnut-colored, with a shy smile like a little boy's. Reverend Smith had always been afraid that Sammy would never be anything more than a cute puppy that delighted in chasing a thrown stick and catching it.

"Seemed like he was the one who suffered the most when Poppa and Momma died," Reverend Smith said thoughtfully, looking through the rearview mirror at Louis. "Something seemed to have gone out of him then and he never got it back."

"I used to try and and tell him that he had to learn to be a little mean to get along in this world, Joshua. Last time I saw him, it was so sad. He was living in this rundown shack. Had to get his water from a faucet out in the yard. Didn't even have electric lights in the shack. But he still had that smile, you know, but it wasn't as big and bright as it used to be, but he couldn't see that.

"He was proud that I was teaching school in Memphis and said that as soon as he made a little money he was going to move to Memphis and go to night school and finish up his high-school diploma. I'd heard lies like that before and I blew up at him. I asked him when he was going to stop fooling himself, 'cause the last person who ever got off the Wellington plantation with their life was Tremble. I told him he had a child now and if he couldn't think about himself and Leora, at least think about Daniel. I said I was going to call his bluff and that he could get in the car with me right then and come to Memphis. I'd pay Wellington whatever he said Sammy owed, and he, Leora, and Daniel could come live with me until he got on his feet.

"But he just smiled that smile, shook his head, and said he couldn't do that. I felt sorry for Leora. She looked like she was going to cry." He sighed. "I feel bad now. I just washed my hands of Sammy after that. Maybe if I'd stayed in touch, he would've changed his mind."

"Don't second-guess yourself like that," Carlotta put in. "You know as well as I do that you can't help somebody who won't help themselves."

"You got a point, Lotty. I just wish I could figure out if Sammy gave up or just never got started."

It was almost ten o'clock when Reverend Smith turned off Highway 61 onto a narrow county road that began winding up into the hills of northern Mississippi.

"Nothing's changed," Louis commented, looking through the window.

Reverend Smith wasn't sure. Once the trees growing out of the hillsides had marked that wide area he called home and there had been something restful in seeing the smoke curling desultorily from the chimneys of houses hidden among the hills. Now the trees and hills were merely trees and hills.

As they neared the crest of a hill he saw a large old pine, its limbs as big around as some trees, and one stout limb stretching the entire breadth of the highway like the arm of God.

"See that tree up ahead, Carl? That big one coming over the highway?"

"Yes, sir," Carl said, sitting forward in the seat.

"They used to hang Negroes from that limb."

"Used to!" Louis exclaimed. "Probably still do."

The car sped beneath the tree and Reverend Smith looked down into the valley.

"Can you see the house?" Louis asked eagerly.

Reverend Smith let his eyes go over the valley to the base of the next hill. The house was there, somewhere, but he wasn't sure he would recognize it, or want to. Nothing had changed, except him, and though everything looked and felt familiar, it was the familiarity of an old coat he didn't want to wear anymore.

"When I was a boy," he said to Carl, "I used to drive a mule and wagon over this road, and it wasn't paved then, either."

Louis chuckled warmly. "I remember you and me riding over this way just on muleback more than once, hunting possum, raccoon, rabbit, and anything else that had some meat on it. I was a little bitty boy."

Reverend Smith laughed. "I didn't think you remembered that."

"Your poppa knew what to do with a rifle, Carl," Louis continued, grinning. "I'd ride behind him on the mule carrying the gunnysack and he'd suddenly stop the mule, point that rifle up in the air, and boom! Down would come a squirrel! I'd ask him, 'Joshua, how you know that squirrel was up there?' You remember what you'd say, Joshua?"

"I said, 'You just got to know what to look for.' "

Louis laughed again. "I never have forgotten that. Knowing what to look for eventually got me a job as principal of the largest Negro high school in Memphis." He laughed again.

The road had leveled off now and after going around a deep curve, there was the sign: WELCOME TO OUICHITTA, POP. 5,468.

"This is where your daddy comes from," Reverend Smith called to Carl.

He slowed the car to thirty miles per hour as they came onto the main street.

"If you want to go on out to the plantation, I think I can probably find the way to where Sammy lived," Louis suggested.

"I thought we'd go on out to the homeplace first. When I talked to Dallas last night, I told him we'd stop there first."

Reverend Smith was surprised at his indifference driving through the business section of the town. He did turn his head to see if the general store was still there. It was.

"That store right there," he said to Carl, "used to keep

a big jar in the window filled with alcohol in which they'd put the ears or private parts of any Negro they lynched."

"Reverend Smith!" Carlotta protested. "What do you want to tell him something like that for?"

"It's all right, Momma," Carl said softly. "It's part of my education."

"Education, my foot!" she said derisively. "I don't know why your daddy wanted to make up a tale like that."

"Didn't make it up," Reverend Smith said simply. "You don't know what it was like for us up in these hills."

Once they were through the town, Reverend Smith accelerated.

"You think you'll remember where the turnoff is?" Louis wanted to know.

"Reckon we're about to find out," Reverend Smith chuckled.

He almost missed it, though, because he was looking for a dirt road, not a gravel one.

"Well, look-a-here!" Louis joked. "Negroes riding on gravel now. Another hundred years and they might get the road paved."

Reverend Smith slowed the car as it crunched over the gravel. He passed a cabin, and a woman standing on the porch, as if trapped in a painting, raised her arm in a desultory wave. He waved back.

Everyone in the car was silent now, as if each revolution of the car's wheels was taking them to the matrix of all their lives. Trees lined each side of the road, silent witnesses to all that had been and would be.

"Ain't that the church?" Louis asked.

Reverend Smith didn't recognize the white-painted building with the stained-glass windows at first.

"They put a steeple on it, too," Louis said.

"The taller the steeple, the lower the religion," Reverend Smith mumbled, not remembering that he was

194

echoing his father and Brother Emory. "That's where I preached my first sermon, Carl. I was the same age you are now."

Quickly now the tall, overpowering pine trees marking the beginning of the property Tremble had wrested from his master came up on the left like ancient monuments marking quiet victories.

"Here we are," Louis said in a hushed voice.

Reverend Smith made a left turn onto a rutted dirt road and there, almost a half-mile in, sat the house, hunched and worn at the foot of the hill.

"And that's where your Uncle Louis and I were born."

Reverend Smith wished he could know what Carl was seeing, or more, what he was feeling.

"Dallas sure has let the place run down," Louis observed.

There had once been fields of cotton and clean rows of vegetables to the north and west of the house. Now the rusted bodies of cars and trucks were stacked haphazardly over the fields as if it were a prehistoric burial ground. The roof of the barn had collapsed and timbers pointed up toward the sky at odd angles like arms of petitioners asking God for mercy. The house looked abandoned, with odd pieces of wood nailed over broken windows, bricks lying on the roof from the broken chimney, and weeds growing up to the edge of the porch.

Reverend Smith brought the car to a stop next to a rust-spotted truck with a wooden flatbed. They had arrived, and everyone seemed to be waiting for him to get out of the car first.

He wasn't sure he wanted to. It had been thirty years since Reverend Smith had seen Dallas, thirty years since he had come from Atlanta and taken Louis away, Dallas standing on the porch yelling and threatening to get his gun.

"What th' hell you think you doing, taking that boy away

from me? You gon' turn him into a sissy like you. Gon'
make him think he's too good to get his hands dirty, gon'
make him think he's better than me like you think you
are."

Sammy had stood in the doorway, that silly smile on his
face. That was the last thing Reverend Smith remembered
seeing before he turned his back on Dallas and said, "Let's
go, Louis," and the two of them, him twenty-six and Louis
sixteen, had walked quietly up the road down which he
had now just driven, and it was more than a walk into town
to catch the train, because he knew that he could never
come back except in remembering.

But he had and the returns in memory had been so
much better than this presence of decay which gave memory the appearance of delusion, and present mocked past,
threatening to deprive him of memory and his son of
legacy.

Reverend Smith saw the front door of the house open
and he opened the car door and stepped out onto the brittle
autumn earth.

A gaunt man in bib overalls a size too big came to the
edge of the porch and stared, one hand shading his eyes
from the weak autumn sun.

"Joshua? Is that you?" came a hoarse voice.

Reverend Smith flinched. Dallas? he thought. Dallas? as
if repeating the name would cause the figure on the porch
to be transformed into flesh and sinew he would recognize.
Dallas? Dallas?, the name echoing through him as if he were
wandering lost in a dense wood.

Carlotta, Carl, and Louis were standing behind him now,
and he did not know if they were hiding, or wanting a more
active protection as Louis exclaimed, "Oh, my God!"

The figure on the porch dropped his hand from his eyes.
"That is you, ain't it? And that's Louis, too, ain't it?" And

his face opened into a wide and toothless grin as he stepped stiffly from the porch and started across the yard.

Reverend Smith walked through the gate and he grinned, not because there was any happiness in this moment but because he did not want his brother's grin to be like a bird whose flight was ended by a windowpane where none should have been.

As Dallas came closer Reverend Smith could see the stubble of a white beard on a gaunt black face, could see thin wrists and oversized skeletal hands protruding from the tattered sleeves of a wool shirt, and then there were long arms spreading like the wings of ancient nightmares and those arms gathered him in and with his head coming barely to the chest of his older brother, he felt like the little boy there had never been space or time for him to be and he wrapped his arms around Dallas's waist and Dallas said his name again and again and again and from the way his voice cracked, Reverend Smith knew that Dallas was crying and tears came to his eyes, too.

Then Louis was there and the man with the long arms as long as life encircled Louis, encircling them both, the three brothers clinging to each other, and Reverend Smith bit back the tears of anger at what should've been, unable to wholly accept this present embrace because it made him know just how deep an emptiness could be.

He eased himself from Dallas's arm and putting on a smile, beckoned Carlotta and Carl to come closer and as Dallas released Louis and moved next to Reverend Smith to greet his sister-in-law and nephew, Reverend Smith's nostrils flared imperceptibly and he wondered why he hadn't smelled the whiskey on Dallas's breath before.

"You sho' got a nice-looking family, Joshua," Dallas commented, grinning, after hugging Carlotta and Carl. "This here is your last-born, ain't it?"

Reverend Smith nodded.

"Thought so. Sammy said you had two. Believe he told me once something about you had a boy in the army?"

"He's stationed in Germany."

"Sho' 'nuf!" Dallas exclaimed with delight. "Well, you don't know how good it makes me feel that you brung your family with you. Sho' does make me feel proud!" With his grin like a clown's face, he turned to Louis. "Louie, you look like you been eating high off the hog."

"And you look like the hog ran off," Louis shot back, smiling.

Everyone laughed.

"Hard times done come to ol' Dallas," he said. "But we can talk about that later. Leora be waiting on y'all, I know."

"Maybe I'd better go up and see if I can find the old cemetery," Reverend Smith suggested. "Leora said that's where she wanted Sammy buried."

Dallas looked at him blankly, started to say something, then mumbled, "We bes' see Leora."

They returned to the car as Dallas got in his truck. After a moment of anxiety when it appeared that the truck wouldn't start, it coughed into life and backfired loudly. Reverend Smith followed the truck down the dirt road.

"Which brother is that, Daddy?" Carl asked as the car turned onto the gravel road.

"My oldest," Reverend Smith said noncommittally.

"That's the one that ran off with all the money after your mother died?"

"What?" Louis exclaimed. "What's this boy talking about, Joshua?"

"Oh, it's nothing," Reverend Smith responded. "You were too little to know anything about it, and from the looks of Dallas now, he's paying the price for it."

"He's paying for something," Louis agreed. "He looks like Death playing hooky from the graveyard."

Carl giggled.

"It's not funny!" Reverend Smith said more angrily than he intended.

As the car followed the truck onto the highway leading into Ouichitta, Reverend Smith began allowing the memories in and each time he started to say, "Do you remember . . . ," he stopped, because there was no one in the car who would, not even something as simple as the wagon ruts of autumn frozen in a paralysis of memory all through the winter, something as simple as the sight of a lantern on a wagon as it moved along the road at night like the ghost of a one-eyed cat, and what he had told Carl and would tell him would never be what he knew.

They went slowly through Ouichitta, turning onto a narrower paved road on each side of which lay fields where dead cotton stalks stuck out of the ground like unanswered prayers. In the fields, a few people, long sacks dragging the ground, were bent over the stalks.

"Scrapping time," Louis said. "Bet you don't know nothing about scrapping time, do you, Carl?"

"Not firsthand," Carl said, "but I believe Daddy told me that when all the cotton was picked, some people went back over the fields looking for any little bit that might still be on the stalks—the scrappings. If I remember right, Daddy said a good scrapper might get enough to make a bale."

"Joshua!" Louis exclaimed. "I see you brought this boy up right!"

Reverend Smith chuckled with pride.

"But I don't know why I said that," Louis continued, a tinge of embarrassment in his voice. "I haven't brought mine up like that. Fact is, I haven't told them a thing about scrapping time or anything else about growing up down here. Guess I want to remember as little as possible myself."

Reverend Smith turned left off the highway onto a one-lane dirt road, following Dallas's truck past gray shacks where children stood in the yard, their eyes fixed on the shiny black car and while Reverend Smith could not say that he had ever looked so poor, those eyes. Those eyes!

"Is this the Wellington plantation, Daddy?"

"This is it," he said as if confirming their presence at a vulgar shrine. "This is the Wellington plantation."

The dirt road changed to faint ruts in a field of grasses as they followed the truck further and further back into the plantation where there were more trees than open, cultivated fields.

"Sammy didn't even make a go of it as a sharecropper," Louis commented.

"You see, Carl," Reverend Smith began, peering through the rearview mirror at the eager open face of his son, "a good sharecropper gets good land and a lot of it to cultivate. If the boss gives you a cabin out here where there's nothing but trees, it means you didn't produce as much as you were supposed to when you had good land. So he puts you out here and tells you to clear some new ground and make a crop."

Louis grunted. "And some of these trees look like they been here since slavery time. It would take a whole lot of dynamite and a bulldozer to clear some of this. It's a good thing we went to see Dallas first, because Sammy wasn't living out here the last time I saw him."

The weeds were higher now and any semblance of a road had vanished. Reverend Smith followed the truck slowly and just as he was beginning to wonder if he should take the car any deeper into the dark forest, Dallas made a right turn and brought the truck to a stop.

It was a moment before Reverend Smith saw the tiny cabin beneath the tall pine and oak trees. As he got out of the car, the door of the cabin opened and a woman with skin the deep brown of a broad and slow-moving river came out.

"Well, I see you made it," she called, smiling. "And ain't that nice? You brought Lotty and who's that? That can't be Josh."

"This is my baby boy, Carl," Reverend Smith said.

"He's the one I never met. And Louis! Lawd, look at you!"

From the happiness in her voice, the smile on her face, and the warmth of her hugs and kisses to each of them, one would never have thought that her husband had died.

"Daniel!" she called into the house. "Bring some chairs out here!"

In a moment a tall boy, skin as sleekly black as a crow's wing, brought chairs onto the porch.

"Boy, if you aren't the spittin' image of your grandfather, my name ain't Louis Smith! Don't he look like Poppa, Joshua?"

Reverend Smith nodded, too amazed to speak. After the newest member of the family was introduced to his kin, Leora motioned for everybody to sit, apologizing to Carl and Dallas that there weren't enough chairs.

"That's all right. I can sit here on the step," Carl said.

"Maybe you should go in the house there with Daniel," Leora suggested. "Take him inside, Daniel."

Daniel shook his head.

Leora started to protest, then stopped. "Well, us grownups got to talk."

"They can stay as far as I'm concerned," Reverend Smith put in.

"Thas all right," Daniel said, "I'll go for a walk. You want to come?" he asked Carl.

Carl looked from his younger and taller cousin to his father and shook his head.

Daniel disappeared around the corner of the house and after a long silence, Leora took Reverend Smith's hand and squeezed it. "I'm glad you're here, Joshua. I know everything's gon' be all right now. I'm glad I called you."

"Was me told you to," Dallas spoke up from the edge of the porch. "You wasn't gon' call him if I hadn't told you it would be all right."

Leora nodded. "That's true. I have to admit that I was a little afraid you wouldn't come."

"I knowed he come," Dallas said with conviction. "I knowed he come."

Leora squeezed Reverend Smith's hand tighter. "It ain't really hit me yet, you know. I keep expecting to see Sammy come walking along the path, smiling like always." She smiled and shook her head. "I ain't never seen no smile like Sammy's. Sometimes when things got really bad, I'd just look at him and see that smile and feel that we'd come through somehow. And we always did. He smiled like he knowed some secret that he couldn't tell nobody. Long as it made him smile, I didn't care what it was."

Reverend Smith's fingers were beginning to hurt and he wanted to ease his hand from hers, but didn't, knowing that she was trying to work up to saying something.

Leora stopped talking and in the silence, he remembered that she was one to whom he could say, "Do you remember?" He had known her almost since she was born, had taught her in Sunday school and baptized her when she joined church, and married her to Sammy. Her hair was still too short for a curling iron, so it was straightened and brushed back from her forehead. Her round eyes were as eager as ever and looking at her made him think of birds' songs at false dawn on a spring morning.

"It's just so good to see you, Joshua," she repeated softly, and for the first time, he heard the strain, not only of Sammy's death but a life lived believing in a smile.

She gave a little laugh. "I be crying in a minute. So let me get on with it. I reckon Dallas didn't tell you."

Dallas looked away, ashamed. "I'se sorry, Leora. It just didn't seem right to tell'em the minute they got out of the car."

"So you decided to wait until they got out of the car at my house."

Dallas lowered his head.

She nodded as if she'd known that this is how it would be. She opened her mouth to speak, stopped, and then said, "It ain't nothing bad. I guess I'm just ashamed, that's all. And don't know what I got to be 'shamed about."

"I'll tell him," Dallas said.

"You just keep your lips pressed together, Dallas. Joshua?" Her voice broke and she dropped his hand and covered her face as she began sobbing violently.

Carlotta got up, put her arms around Leora, and led her inside the house.

The men were left alone on the porch, with Reverend Smith, Louis, and even Carl, staring at Dallas sitting on the edge of the porch staring into the woods.

"What's going on?" Louis asked, not bothering to hide the contempt in his voice.

Dallas turned sideways to them. "Y'all gon' hate me when I tells you."

"Damn!" Louis exploded. "Will you be a man instead of acting like a little boy who peed in his pants?"

Reverend Smith was surprised to see a tear trail down Dallas's withered face.

"You right, Louis. You right." He nodded and cleared his throat. "I'm gon' tell you the whole story. Leora don't know this part." He stopped. "Sammy, well, Sammy, he didn't die of no heart attack. It was some bad moonshine. And he wasn't croppin' on the Wellington plantation, neither. This here house is on the Wellington property, I reckon, but it was all falling down and him and me fixed it up just a couple of months ago after Sammy got kicked off the plantation. He was so far in debt and wouldn't work either. Mr. Wellington tol' him that he wasn't running no welfare office, 'cause Sammy didn't even pretend to be trying to make a crop. Leora and Daniel tried, but they couldn't make it, just the two of'em. So we fixed up this place here. Don't nobody come back here. Not even white folks. Niggers talk about ghosts back here from slavery times." He sighed. "Might as well tell it all and be done with it. I ain't doing too hot myself. Doctor say it syphilis, say I done had it for years and ain't nothing can be done now. My insides is rotting away. So, I been selling the land back at the place a little at a time just to try to keep a little food on the table for myself and Sammy and Leora and the boy. All them cars you seen there is from a white man who bought it to use as a junkyard. And some white lawyer in town bought the hillside back of the house. Say it might be worth something one of these days."

"You sold the cemetery?" Reverend Smith exclaimed, incredulous.

"Aw, I knowed I couldn't have sold it if he knowed there was dead folks there, so I took down that old fence and took a sledge to them old headstones. They was all crumbly anyway, and the cemetery was growed over."

"My God!" Reverend Smith exclaimed. "My God! Do you know what you've done?"

"I knowed what I done," he answered sullenly. "I been

trying to keep food on the table. That's what I done."

"Why didn't you call one of us?" Louis wanted to know. "We would've sent you and Sammy money."

Dallas just shook his head. "Let me finish my story." He cleared his throat again and resumed. "Knowing that that white lawyer wasn't going to be doing nothing with the property, me and Sammy built a still up there." He stopped and chewed at his lower lip. "We had to do something. I'd done sold all the property 'cepting for the house and it ain't worth nothing now. The money from all the property being sold was gone. Bossman at the Wellington plantation tol' Sammy he had to go. We had to do something!" He looked up at Reverend Smith, a plea in his eyes. "You can understand that, can't you, Joshua?"

"Go on with your story," was all Reverend Smith said.

Dallas nodded and hurried on. "Neither one of us never made 'shine in our lives, but we'd sho' drunk our share and been around stills enough to see how it was done. We didn't have one of them fancy stills with copper pipes and steam. Didn't have the kind of money that takes. We just had us a little ol' black-pot still and the first batch we made turned out good. Sol' it right away." He lowered his head and started to weep. "Don't know what went wrong with the next batch. I had a feeling about it, too, but didn't say nothing, 'cause I didn't think nothing of the feeling. Sammy drank some of that batch and next thing I knowed he was lying on the ground, twisting and turning." His sobs came harder now. "He was crying and screaming for me to help him and I couldn't do nothing! I couldn't do nothing! I couldn't even think of how the Lawd's Prayer go."

His crying slowed. He sniffed, wiped at his nose, and continued. "That's the part Leora don't know about. I tol' her me an' him was doing some work and he had a heart attack and was dead fo' he hit the ground. What she couldn't tell you is that she ain't got no money for the undertaker. And I ain't neither. Sammy laying up in the house there. Leora had to sleep with a dead man last night, 'cause wasn't no other place for him."

"Give me the keys to your car, Joshua," Louis said angrily, getting up. "I'll go get the undertaker and bring him out here."

"Can't," Reverend Smith said quietly.

"What do you mean?" Louis wanted to know.

"Can't," Reverend Smith repeated. "The undertaker could tell just by looking that Sammy didn't die of a heart attack. He'd know what killed Sammy, and he wouldn't have no choice but to call the police and they been knowing Dallas for a long time."

"So what're you saying?" Louis asked quietly, sitting back down.

Reverend Smith stood up and sighed. "You and Dallas take the truck and go to the lumberyard and get some lumber. I'll need a hammer, some nails, maybe a plane and some sandpaper, I reckon."

He gave Louis the lengths to which he needed the boards cut and telling Carl to go in the kitchen where his mother and Leora were, Reverend Smith went inside.

Sammy lay on a bed to the left of the door. Leora had folded his arms across his chest in imitation of the peace of death, but the twisted and agonized lines in that face spoke only of an unutterable pain.

Reverend Smith sat on the edge of the bed and looked down at Sammy. He ran his hand over his hair as if stroking a sleeping child, as if he were eight years old again and had begged Momma to let Sammy sleep in the bed with him, now that Sue Ann was dead, and finally she relented and he helped Sammy out of his clothes, slipped the nightshirt over his head, and after tucking him in bed, told him a story, stroking his hair as he was doing now, stroking his hair and telling him the story about Samuel whom God called when he was a little boy to be the one to choose the King of Israel, and about Joshua leading the children of Israel to the Promised Land and how he blew on the ram's horn and the walls came tumbling down, and Sammy was always soon asleep, a smile on his face and Joshua who had already at that age made the box for Sue Ann and said the words over her grave, who had sorrow (even, then) as tiny and plentiful as stars, had been so jealous of that smile, had knelt beside the bed to say his prayers, asking God if he could ever have a smile like that and now, stroking Sammy's hair, now with rigor mortis having locked Sammy's face into a mask of perpetual agony, now he let the tears come, not in sorrow nor in anger but in obedience to a will and a justice that would be forever beyond him.

When Louis and Dallas returned with the wood and tools, he refused their offer of help, telling them there was nothing for them to do, and sent them inside. He was surprised to look up a moment later to see Carl standing on the porch looking solemnly at him. Carl gave a small smile and came off the porch and held the pine board Reverend Smith had been trying to steady to nail into the plywood bottom.

And Reverend Smith began talking, without purpose, almost rambling, the memories tumbling over each other like rocks in an avalanche—the making of the box for Sue Ann, Tremble, Brother Emory, and how a solitary crow looked like a messenger from Hell on a cold gray winter day, and frozen ruts and the feel of a plow tongue as it sank into moist spring earth early in the morning. He talked, not knowing then if Carl listened, not knowing if he could hear in that place where the blood flowed and memory was a heartbeat, and he could talk only because he dared not hope that he was being heard, and lacked enough pride at that moment to wish that he were being heard. He talked and hammered and before he knew it, or knew how, the box was finished, and he and Carl carried it into the house and had started to lift Sammy into it when Daniel walked through the door and without being asked or being told, Carl moved to the side to let Daniel take hold of the feet, and straining his slim, young body, lift the body heavy with death into the box. Carl moved forward and helped his cousin lift the foot of the box, and once they lowered it to the ground outside, Reverend Smith nailed on the top.

"I know where we can lower him down," Daniel offered timidly. "It's a special place. Leastways, it is to me. Don't nobody knows about it 'cepting me."

"Why don't you show us?" Reverend Smith said gently.

Reverend Smith and Carl followed him behind the house and onto a tiny trail among trees as long as memory and Reverend Smith, remembering, knew even before Daniel led them into a clearing where no grass grew, and at the far end, the earth was like a sunken tub.

"Don't nobody ever come here," Daniel said. "I likes it here," he continued softly. "I likes it here a lot."

Reverend Smith looked at the boy and smiled, nodding his head. "I think your father would like it here, too," and he continued to himself, *and maybe Madame Couseau can take the misery out of his face, and out of his heart, and out of his soul.*

"You go on back to the house and see if your Uncle Dallas has a shovel in his truck. Would you like to dig the grave?"

The boy nodded eagerly. "Yes, suh, Uncle Joshua. Thank you."

"You go on now."

And so it was done as the light withdrew from day and the stars appeared, crowding into the blackening sky to witness another burial in that place where the lowering down had been only at night and no one but stars and trees and God remembered who was buried there and why and when.

Reverend Smith, Carlotta, Carl, and Louis drove back to Memphis immediately afterward and the next morning, he and Louis returned to take Leora and Daniel to live with Louis, and to put Dallas in a hospital where he died six months later.

Reverend Smith blinked his eyes and was once again staring down at himself through the eyes of God, staring down at an old black man, his hair as white as clouds.

He blinked his eyes again and was staring at the painting again and saw it now as his face and Sammy's and Dallas's and Poppa's and Momma's and Madame Couseau's and Boxer's and all the black faces that only the stars remembered and he got on his knees and thanked God for the trembling in his hands, for the tiny pains in his body telling him that death was nigh, that death was coming on like the morning star leading the way toward day.

And he blinked his eyes again and was surprised to find that he was sitting in his study as he had sat on that winter day staring at the painting and wondering (then) as he did not wonder now, who he was and had been, not wondering now about the son who came from the father but was not of the father for that could not be so.

He got up slowly and made his way down the hallway to the bedroom where Carlotta sat up in her bed, reading. Reverend Smith stood in the doorway for a moment, unseen, and looked at her.

When she finally felt his gaze on her, she turned, and instead of frowning as he feared, instead of asking him why he was standing there and staring at her, she smiled, and his eyes wanted to look away as if he were shy and a bride again, but he smiled and allowed his eyes to be held by hers and he saw her blush a pale and faded crimson.

His smile, broad and full now, reached out and gathered her to him as his arms could do no longer, and held her to him in ways his arms had never done, and then, at the very edge of that moment coming on like the morning star giving a benediction to the night, he began again.